ATTACK BY MAGIC

DRAGON'S GIFT THE VALKYRIE BOOK 4

LINSEY HALL

For Alison, one of my favorite Wonder Women.

1

I strode down the busy street in Edinburgh, the midday sun bright in the sky. Cade walked next to me, towering over the other supernaturals that bustled around us. I couldn't help but glance at him appreciatively as we stopped in front of an old bookstore.

I gripped the stone in my pocket, a charm that would allow us to pass through the enchanted bookshop and reach The Vaults, an underground street beneath the castle. Shady supernaturals practiced dark magic in The Vaults. It wasn't my scene, but we needed answers, and this was the place to get them.

Right now, I wanted to know more about the Rebel Gods we'd fought two days ago.

"Do you know where we'll find Oya?" I asked Cade. We hoped his old mercenary friend would be able to help identify one of the Rebel Gods who'd gotten away. He'd taken my sister with him, and I'd stop at nothing to get her back.

"We'll have to ask around. Her operations used to be in Magic's Bend, but she recently moved here."

I nodded, then opened the door to the bookshop. The scent of leather and paper wafted out.

"Welcome." An old woman's voice echoed through the cluttered space. There was no one there, though. Just the old, cluttered house... which, oddly enough, could talk. If I hadn't had the enchanted stone in my pocket, the house would have quickly evicted us.

"Hi," I said.

"Don't touch anything."

I smiled. "I won't."

Cade chuckled. We weaved through piles of books stacked along the walls. I glanced longingly at the books. Eventually, I'd have the time to read. But until I rescued Rowan, my favorite hobby would have to take a back seat.

Near the rear of the store, we stopped in front of a portal that glowed with shimmery light. I glanced up at Cade. "Ready?"

"Ready."

He took my hand, the strong press of his palm making my breath catch in my throat. We'd shared kisses and hot looks, but that hadn't been enough to cool my desire.

I wanted Cade. Badly.

But we were busy trying to save Rowan from the Rebel Gods, which meant fighting one battle after another, and spending every non-fighting moment licking our wounds and healing.

One day, though. One day I'd climb him like a tree.

Today was not that day, though.

I followed him through the portal, my hand in his.

It was dark on this side. I glanced up, catching sight of the night sky and stars between the roofs of the buildings. It was an illusion—in reality, there was only the rock of the mountain overhead. But it was nice that they at least tried to make it feel less like the giant cave it was.

"It's never day in here?" I asked.

Cade shook his head. "Takes too much magic to make that much light. Stars are easier."

Made sense.

I studied the street that we'd stepped onto. It was a narrow, cobblestone lane that wound slightly uphill and was bordered on either side by old shops built right into the stone. They looked like they'd been built in a normal fashion, until you looked closely and realized that they'd been hewn from the rock itself.

On my right, an old man stepped out of a shop that sold pygmy toads. Amos. He was stooped and bald, and his grouchy gaze brightened at the sight of Cade and me.

"You again!" he said.

"Us again." Cade smiled at him. "I don't suppose you can tell me where I might find Oya?"

Amos's brow furrowed and he grumbled, "Mercenaries are troublemakers. But seeing as how you helped me fight off the mobsters who wanted to shake me down, I suppose I can help." He glanced behind him, making eye contact with a hundred little toads who sat in his shop window. They all gazed at him with bulging green eyes, and I'd have sworn their gazes were conveying some kind of message. He turned back to us. "Yes, my toads insist. You protected them, after all."

I grinned, imagining myself as Bree Blackwood, protector of pygmy toads. In reality, I'd just seen some masked men kick down his door a few weeks ago and hadn't wanted old Potts to get hurt. But saving pygmy toads was cool, too.

"You can find Oya on Lucifer's Lane," Amos said. "She runs her operations out of the office over the Dark Dragon Pub. Only been there a few weeks, but already there are more bar fights."

"Thank you," Cade said.

Amos grumbled and nodded to us, then turned and went back into his shop, singing "Hello, my lovelies" to his pygmy toads as he went.

We hoofed it up the street, which was lit by the golden glow of old-fashioned gas lamps. Dark magic permeated the air here, smelling of all sorts of unsavory things like old socks and wet mold. There was the occasional whiff of light magic as well, though, which generally smelled and felt nicer. The whole place wasn't bad, after all. Just most of it.

I glanced at my watch. "We only have a few hours till the meeting at the Protectorate."

"We'll make it," he said.

"Good." We needed to be at that meeting. We were gathering all our allies and friends to help us figure out how to track the Rebel Gods who'd stolen my sister Rowan years back. She'd been so close when we'd fought them two days ago, but I'd lost her.

I wouldn't lose her this time.

We just needed Oya to help us identify one of the Rebel Gods Cade had thought he'd recognized. He planned to share his memories with her and hoped she'd be able to give us more info.

We passed all sorts of supernaturals—shifters, demons with serrated horns, goblins, and witches with warts on their noses. So cliché. Some of the warts didn't even look real. Almost as if they were fashion statements.

We turned left onto Lucifer's Lane, an even darker alley that was cast in shadow. Most of the gas lamps were out, and the sidewalk gleamed slickly with some kind of fluid I didn't want to identify.

"I think I'll stick with the Whisky and Warlock," I muttered.

"It is the preferable pub," Cade murmured.

A man leaning against the wall in the shadows glowered at us, but didn't give us any trouble as we hurried by.

The door to the Dark Dragon was small and sturdy looking. Cade pulled it open and ducked under the low lintel. I followed, not needing to stoop.

As soon as we entered, the feeling of hostility rolled over me. The place was low ceilinged and dimly lit. A smoky fire belched into the room, surrounding the tiny wooden tables with a hazy gray cloud. Men and women of all species sat around tables, playing cards and drinking. They had nothing in common except an aura of danger.

Then they all turned to look at us, as if the door to the Dark Dragon didn't open often. About twenty pairs of eyes gleamed through the darkness, riveted to the doorway where we stood.

"This is a private club," growled a large goblin to the left of me. I'd never seen one as big as him—normally they were only a few feet tall. This guy was over six feet, and his wrinkled green skin and hawked nose were the only indicator of his species.

"We're here to see Oya," Cade said.

"Well, she's not interested in seeing you," the goblin said.

"I'm sure that's wrong." Cade grinned, a lethal slice of a smile that would have made me shiver if it'd been directed at me.

Here, in this den of thieves and murderers, he looked right at home, as comfortable as if he had his feet kicked up in front of his own fire. If I hadn't known what a good guy he was, I'd have thought he was their leader.

The whole room roiled with powerful magic, but there was an even stronger signature overhead. It sounded like a battle cry and felt like the press of cold steel against my neck. Oya was another warrior god, just like Cade.

"I think she's upstairs," I murmured. "I feel her magic."

Cade nodded slightly. "We'll go for the stairs. Mercenaries are protective, so we may have to fight."

"I'd be delighted."

Cade took one step forward, and everyone in the room surged to their feet.

Jeesh, they took this "private club" thing seriously.

I drew my sword and shield from the ether, and Cade did the

same. I could handle this with magic, but honestly, I was in the mood for a tussle.

"Oya!" Cade stepped toward the stairs.

The room erupted in a roar. A red-skinned demon in front of me hurled a fireball at us. I raised my shield just in time, and the flame crashed against it.

I sprinted for him, slicing down with my sword before he could power up another blast. My blade cleaved a gash in his shoulder, and he spun away from me, gripping the wound.

Next to me, Cade was a whirlwind, his blade flying so fast I could hardly see it. He never delivered a killing blow. No doubt Oya would disapprove of us killing her mercenaries.

I felt the next attacker more than saw him and whirled, my blade outstretched. The huge goblin was only three feet away, his giant black blade raised to strike. My sword sliced him across the belly, and acid green blood spilled forth. He roared, bringing his blade down toward my head.

I hoisted my shield just as his sword crashed against it. The metal rang from the blow, and my arm ached.

I kicked, nailing him in his wounded stomach, and he stumbled back.

A woman with long fangs and pale white skin raced for me, claws outstretched. They were twelve inches long and gleamed white.

Shit.

Poison coated those lethal claws, no doubt. I stashed my sword in the ether and drew one of my daggers, then hurled it at the woman.

It plunged into her shoulder right before she reached me, and she screeched, falling backward. I drew my sword again, spinning to find Cade.

A group of three-horned demons charged me. I raised my shield, ready to deflect their blows.

"Stop!" The voice rang with power.

All of our attackers halted in their tracks.

My gaze flew to the narrow stairs. A beautiful black woman stood on the lowest step, her hair closely cropped and her dark eyes sharp. She wore dark brown leather pants and heavy boots. Her strappy top was cut from the same leather, but threaded through with copper embellishments. Power rolled off of her—the sound of a war cry and the cold press of steel that I'd sensed earlier.

"Oya." Cade grinned. "Good to see you."

Her lips flattened. Yep, she was clearly annoyed. But there was pleasure in her dark eyes when she looked at Cade. I saw it in my own eyes when I looked in the mirror after being around him.

A demon stepped forward, his gaze on Oya. "We tried to stop them, Your Eminence."

"Cade is an exception to the rule." She flicked her fingers in a come-here motion. "Follow me. And someone bring us some drinks."

I glanced at all the mercenaries, each of whom looked at us suspiciously. But they did as their mistress commanded, parting to allow us to follow Oya up the stairs.

We joined her in another small, low-ceilinged room. The decor was Spartan—just a table with chairs and some weapons leaning against the walls. Papers were scattered over the tables, and she gathered them into a pile, flipping them upside down.

A job, no doubt.

She glanced up at us as we entered, calmly assessing us with her penetrating eyes.

"What brings you here, Cade?" Her voice was tightly controlled. This was a woman who always won. *Always.* "I thought you said you'd never walk with our kind again."

"I'm done being a mercenary. But I need your help."

Her eyes gleamed with interest as she sat and then propped one ankle on her knee. She leaned back and grinned. "Is that so?"

Cade nodded sharply and then sat, too. I followed, my gaze riveted to Oya. Cade had said she was an African war goddess of the Yoruba people. She'd been his boss once, long ago.

"You abandoned us on a job. Why should I help you now?" she said.

"You were kidnapping children to sell them," he said. "I wanted no part of that."

She smiled, her white teeth gleaming in the dim light. "We weren't. That was the front for our operation, but we weren't."

Strangely enough, I believed her. Oya might lead a band of mercenaries, but her magic didn't feel dark. She had plenty of honor.

Cade looked at her, his gaze hard. Trying to decide if he believed her.

"But you left before you could find out the details of the plan," Oya said. "You never did trust easily, Cade."

Maybe because his family had locked him in a cell when they'd learned he was an Earth-walking god.

"Still, I can't say that I blame you," Oya said. "You never were meant to follow."

"And you were always meant to lead," Cade said.

"And lead I have." She nodded at a bruiser of a man who stood in the doorway, a tray in his hands. His magic smelled of burning rubber.

He hurried in and put the tray of beers on the table.

"That'll be all, Stan," Oya said.

"Aye." He lumbered out, quick for such a big man.

"You've found a new life for yourself at the Protectorate?" she asked.

"I have. And we now have a job that might involve another god."

Her brows rose. "A god? Not an Earth-walking one? I'd have heard if there was another one of us."

"Aye, a Rebel God. His magic made that obvious. I believe he may be a Celtic war god, but I am not sure which one. There are many. And you always knew your gods."

She nodded. "Indeed. And you want me to confirm his identity?"

"Aye, if you can."

"How do you propose to do this?"

He dug into his pocket and raised a clear crystal disk. "A projector."

Hedy, the Protectorate's resident magical genius, had given him the device that would project his memories onto a wall so that others could see them.

Oya nodded appreciatively. "That could work."

"I hope so. You'll help us, then?"

She shrugged. "I can try. If only to prove that I'm not the monster you assumed I was."

"You're ruthless, Oya. How was I to know you didn't intend to sell those children? That you were actually rescuing them?"

"You could have asked. But that kind of trust is outside of your wheelhouse, isn't it? And you'd been wanting to leave the mercenary lifestyle for a while."

"That's true."

The air sang with tension. They'd been friends once, as well as colleagues. But that had changed.

Cade raised the projector again. "Ready?"

Oya nodded.

Cade held the projecting crystal straight out, in front of his face. He closed his eyes, obviously envisioning what he wanted to share with Oya.

An image flashed on the dark wall across from us. It was the scene from two days ago that was burned into my memory—the moment when I'd realized my sister was still alive. That, in fact, she was the powerful woman who had hunted us on behalf of the Rebel Gods. She'd been cursed somehow, because she'd never hurt Ana or me. Not if she had any say in it.

In the image, a massive, horned god wrapped arms around Rowan's waist, and he dragged her into the golden mist of the transport charm. More gold glittered on his horns, and he was a hulking figure. His magic had smelled of sulfur.

The image faded.

Cade turned to Oya. "Anything?"

She frowned, gaze intense. "I think that's Cocidius."

Cade nodded sharply. "Good. I didn't know if it was Cocidius or Segomo. Or even Rudianos. We don't have time to waste hunting the wrong god."

"It's definitely not Segomo or Rudianos. I'd bet money that is Cocidius."

I pulled my phone out of my pocket and typed a short message to Ana, revealing the identity of the Rebel God. She'd spread the word to Florian, the librarian, so he could find everything of interest about Cocidius. Florian didn't have his own phone, as he was a ghost who last walked the earth during the seventeenth century.

"Thank you," Cade said. "And for what it's worth, I'm sorry for doubting you."

Oya inclined her head. "Maybe work on those trust issues some."

As if he couldn't help himself, his gaze landed on me. A tiny light of happiness lit in my chest. He did trust me. At least, mostly. More than Oya.

Cade and I had something. We just had to muddle our way through what it was.

Twenty minutes later, we hurried across the lawn toward the Protectorate castle. We'd hightailed it out of the Vaults and headed straight back through the portal for our meeting with the rest of the gang.

Cade glanced at his watch. "We'll be just in time."

"Good. I want to get started looking for Rowan." I was *itching* to. All the years of searching for her....and we finally had a real clue.

Sunlight glinted off the mullioned glass windows of the castle, a massive structure that I still couldn't believe was my home. If someone had told me I'd be turning in the dust of Death Valley for the cool mist of the Scottish Highlands, I wouldn't have believed them.

But here I was.

As we neared the great double doors that led to the entry hall, Mayhem flew out of the castle and hurtled toward us, her squished pug face beaming with happiness.

She yipped and flew circles around me, her wings moving so fast they were a blur.

"Someone is happy to see you," Cade said.

I reached out and ruffled the fur at the top of her head, which felt like a weird tingle instead of dog fur. One of the hazards of being a ghost, but Mayhem didn't seem to mind.

We entered the castle and headed directly to the round room, where all the important meetings took place.

Technically, I was still in training at the Protectorate Academy, trying to earn my stripes so that I could be admitted to a division and become a full-fledged member. It'd been going pretty well. But now that we'd almost found Rowan, I wasn't sure if there'd be a break in my training. All I knew was that I'd be dedicating every moment to finding her.

We entered the round room, which was mostly full. Judy and Hedy sat next to each other, along with my friends Caro, Ali, and Haris.

But it was Ana and Cass who caught my eye. Cass had come all the way from Magic's Bend to help us track down Rowan. She shot me a grin, her red hair glinting in the light of the sconces. She'd draped her leather jacket over the back of the chair and looked right at home in the Protectorate.

"You discovered the horned Rebel God's identity, I hear?" Jude asked as we sat.

"We did," Cade said. "The Celtic war god Cocidius."

"Florian and Dr. G are finding what info they can," Ana said. "They'll be here soon."

"Dr. G?" I asked.

"Dr. Garriso," Cass said. "I brought him from Magic's Bend. I thought he could help."

"Thank you," I said.

Cass nodded.

Jude leaned forward, her gaze on me. "We're gathered here to find Bree and Ana's sister, and to take out the Rebel Gods. Bree, it will be part of your training."

"What about Ana?" I asked. I was getting all the good opportunities. I didn't want her left out in the cold.

"My magic hasn't manifested," Ana said. "Yours has."

I could hear the wistfulness in her voice—she still didn't know what kind of DragonGod she was.

"Ana will be part of the team. But you, Bree, will lead. With supervision. I've discussed it with Arach and the other division heads. If you save your sister and take out the Rebel Gods, you'll have finished your training. It's an unusually fast training period, but you've come into your powers. And without a doubt, taking out the Rebel Gods would be the greatest trainee accomplishment that this institution has ever seen."

At this point, I only cared about saving my sister. But the idea that Arach, the dragon spirit who presided over the castle, knew about my mission made me feel a bit better. I didn't know if she supported me, but I hoped she did and I liked the possibility of it.

I leaned forward. "All right. If I'm leading this, then here's what I think. Cass, Del, and Nix were never able to track Rowan. She's blocked somehow. But that doesn't mean we can't try to find the Rebel Gods who abducted her. Now that we've destroyed their stronghold in the ether, that means they're probably hiding out in one of their godly realms."

"That makes sense," Jude said. "It takes great magic for a god to walk upon the earth. It'd be easiest for them to recoup in their own realm."

"Exactly," I said. "It's only a matter of time before they create another stronghold. We have to find them before that. So Cade and I will seek Cocidius in his realm." I looked at him. "You think you can find him?"

"With research and a bit of luck, yes. Florian said that he had resources that might help us track him down. Or at least, his realm."

"We do have one thing that might help you," Jude said. "To be used only in a case of sincerest emergency. It is a heavenly transport charm. As you know, regular transport charms don't let you enter or exit another realm. You have to use a portal for that. But we have one—just one—transport stone that would allow you to escape Cocidius's realm if you were in a bind."

"Oh, perfect." Excitement welled in my chest. "This improves our chances even more. We can grab Rowan and run."

"Fighting our way out of a godly realm will be difficult. This will be immensely helpful," Cade said. "Thank you, Jude."

"We've been saving it for an appropriate time. This is it."

"Thank you." I smiled at her, then looked at Cass. "Back at

the Rebel Gods stronghold, you wrestled with the goddess wearing the ancient robes. The one covered with blood. Do you think you can use your magic to track her?"

"I can try."

"I'll go with her," Ana said.

"So will I," Caro said. "Ali and Haris can stay and do research into the third god. Try to find out who he is so we can track him."

Ali and Haris both scowled, likely at the idea of being left behind to do research, but both eventually nodded and grinned.

They were team players, no matter what the job. It made me like them even more.

"You'll get to go into the field to hunt him down if you find some leads," Jude said.

The guys grinned even wider.

"Oh, we'll find leads," Haris said.

Ali grinned. "You can count on us."

"Perfect. We'll split up and see what we can find," I said. "Hopefully, that will be Rowan."

2

The others had just departed the room, leaving only Cade and me, when Florian hurried in, followed by an older man with wispy white hair and a tweed jacket that had patches on the arms.

"Sincerest apologies on our tardiness!" the ghost librarian cried. "We were required to locate some documents, and one was being quite stubborn. Wouldn't come down off the shelf." Florian dropped some books on the table, along with a few rolled up maps.

The old man stepped up to Cade and me and held out his hand. "I'm Dr. Garriso, director of the Museum for Magical History in Magic's Bend. Cassiopeia Clereaux asked me to come and lend my assistance."

I shook his hand. "Thank you for coming."

He nodded as he shook Cade's hand. "My pleasure."

"Come!" Florian said. "Look at what Dr. Garriso found."

We moved over to the table, where Florian had laid out several open books and maps.

"One of my specialties is ancient Celtic religions." He pointed a gnarled finger at a little drawing on one of the book's pages. "As soon as we received the message that the god was Cocidius, I remembered this carving found on Hadrian's Wall."

"The ancient Roman wall that was built between Scotland and England?" I asked.

"Yes. That's where Cocidius was worshipped primarily. He was a more minor god favored by the Celtic poor and the Roman military. Not a high status god."

"Ah, no wonder he has a chip on his shoulder," I said.

"He wants more power. And the idea that the other gods would give some of theirs to the DragonGods rubs him the wrong way," Cade said. "If we want to find him in his realm, where he's no doubt licking his wounds and stoking his rage, we need to find the entrance."

"Exactly." Dr. Garriso nodded. "And I think I have an idea."

"It's somewhere near Hadrian's Wall?" Cade asked.

"Yes," Florian said. "It'll be at the point where the most people worshipped him. His power will be strongest there, able to create a bridge between the human world and his godly one."

"He's a lower god, so his realm should be much easier to access," Dr. Garriso said. "The Celtic gods are very hierarchical. Higher gods occupy larger worlds that are harder to get to. True god realms. Those are the true Celtic afterworlds. But Cocidius owns a realm that is lesser. It's more of a mirror realm —one that is on Earth, layered over top of the world that we know. Those are easier to create, and therefore easier to access."

"Thank fates." I didn't want to be kept away from Rowan by some godly hierarchy that hid her in an inaccessible realm.

"I think I may have found the entrance to his realm. Roughly." Dr. Garriso pointed to several places on the maps. "At these locations, scholars have found ancient carvings of Cocidius, dug into stone by those who once worshipped him."

My gaze followed his fingertip as it traced over the locations.

An idea clicked in my mind. This was like an old-school version of *CSI*. "The entrance will be at the center of all those carvings."

"Exactly," Florian crowed.

"You must go there and find where the magic is strongest," Dr. Garriso said. "Then you can find the entrance to his realm. But be careful. It will be dangerous."

Ha. I was used to dangerous. And to save Rowan, I'd throw myself into hell.

Cade and I left immediately for Hadrian's Wall, each of us wearing a version of Celtic attire so we'd blend in when we arrived. The leather pants and tunic weren't far off what I'd normally wear, fortunately.

Ana, Cass, and Caro had set out twenty minutes before us, following Cass's dragon sense to see if they could find the blood-covered goddess.

"I hope Rowan is with Cocidius." I patted the heavenly transport stone in my pocket as we walked out onto the main lawn. I couldn't wait any longer to find her.

"Don't worry, Bree. We'll get her back."

I smiled at him, and adjusted the small backpack. Each of us carried a pack filled with food and water. We were unsure of what we'd be stepping into in Cocidius's realm, and we wanted to be prepared.

"Ready?" Cade asked.

I nodded, swallowing hard.

Suddenly, my chest felt tight. I was so close to something that I'd wanted for so long, but it brought with it a visceral fear of failure.

I sucked in a ragged breath, trying to calm myself.

Cade hesitated, the transport charm clutched in his hand.

"Are you all right?" Concern shadowed his gaze.

I looked up, breathing raggedly. "Yeah. Yeah."

"You don't look all right."

"I know. Funny how monsters and demons don't bother me a bit, but I'm so close to Rowan and the odds of failure are so great." I shook my head. "It scares the shit out of me."

He pulled me close, tucking me under his chin. I shuddered, leaning into him and absorbing his strength.

"You can do this, Bree. You're the fiercest, most determined person I've ever met. You'll save your sister."

My breathing calmed. Not that I wasn't still scared, but his confidence gave me confidence.

And I loved that he had faith in me. He didn't say that he would help me—that was obvious—just that I could do it.

And I could. I had to.

I squeezed him back and then drew away, my chest looser. My breathing no longer sounded like a wheezy air conditioner.

"Thanks for the talk. Let's do this."

"On three." He counted, then hurled a transportation stone at the ground.

The glittery gray dust billowed up, and I stepped inside. The ether sucked me through space, spitting me out at the edge of a low, broken wall.

Cade appeared at my side, then knelt to study the stones.

It was only four feet tall and about twelve wide. In the two thousand years since it'd been built, time had taken its toll.

"Here's the carving," Cade said.

I bent down to look at the small man holding a sword and shield. It was the best carving of those that Dr. Garriso had found, and was located roughly at the geographical center of all the other carvings.

I touched it, and magic spark through my fingertips. A brief scent of blood hit my nose, followed by the anxiety of waiting for a battle to start.

I shuddered.

That was the *worst.*

I'd only recently started to gain control of my own anxiety over battle—the nerves that made me leap before I looked. But it turned out that one of Cocidius's magical signatures was that same anxiety.

Great.

I stood and turned, taking in my surroundings. Hills rolled out in all directions, some leading back into Scotland and some leading into England. In the distance, near a copse of trees, a broken-down, stone structure hulked behind an earthen mound.

I pointed to it. "Dollars to donuts, that's an old Roman fort."

"Aye, let's check it out."

We set off across the grass. Cool wind rustled my hair back from my face, but it couldn't distract me from the ugly magic that rolled from the fort.

Anxiety rose in my chest, and the scent of blood filled my nose. "That's definitely his magic."

Cade nodded, brow furrowed. "This feels odd."

I climbed to the top of the earthen mound that surrounded the ruined remains of the fort. At the top, I could see that the mound was hexagonal in shape, surrounding the stone foundations of the old fort.

Up close, the crumbled stone building that I'd seen from far away looked like an old square castle.

Cade pointed to it. "That's medieval. Too late for Cocidius's time. But this fort... It's definitely Roman. And the stones that made up the foundation were probably used to create the castle long after the Romans had retreated."

"So they broke apart the fort and used it for their own stuff."

I climbed down off the mound of earth and entered the fort. As soon as I stepped past the walls, magic shivered over my skin.

Anxiety ratcheted up within me, and the scent of blood clouded my senses. "You feel that?"

Cade stepped down into the grassy interior of the fort and shuddered. "The magic is dark here. Definitely his. The Roman soldiers who lived here worshipped him. No question."

"So we're hopefully at the entrance to his realm." I paced the length of the stone foundations of the fort, which only rose a foot off the ground. "We just have to find it."

Cade joined me, pacing through the fort. Birds chirped and the sun shone as I studied the area around me, hoping for a clue.

The whole time, Cade was silent, but I could feel his unease. It was strange, since he rarely seemed to feel anything other than comfort and confidence.

"You all right?" I asked.

"I feel a connection here." He grimaced. "It's unpleasant."

I knelt and studied a tall, slender stone that made up one of the six corners of the hexagonal fort. It extended up above the rest of the broken foundation.

Little hatch marks had been carved into the edge of the stone. They looked kinda familiar and definitely not natural.

"Hey, Cade, come look at this."

He joined me, kneeling at my side. His arm pressed against mine, warm and strong, and I shivered.

I looked at him. He squinted, studying the stone and the carvings.

"What do you think?"

"Ogham script," he said. "Ancient Celtic writing from Ireland. Examples are rare in Britain and Scotland, but not unheard of."

"What does it say?"

He frowned. "Normally Ogham depicted only names. But this... I think it says that the god must stand within the center of the place of worship to ignite the portal."

"Wow, you're good at reading Ogham. All that history study paid off."

"Aye, it did, but in other ways. This, I was born with. Perk of being with the Celts."

I nodded. "Must be a god thing. I understand runes and Old Norse, even though I haven't studied."

"It must." He stood. "The god must stand at the center of the place of worship. I'm not the right god though."

"You can still try. You are a war god, and so is he."

A grin tugged at the corner of his mouth. "You read my mind."

He walked to the center of the hexagonal fort. The castle sat on the far edge to the east, a ghostly structure that looked lonely against the clear blue sky.

Cade stood directly in the middle, waiting for something to happen.

I counted to ten.

Nothing happened.

Damn.

We really needed this to work.

"Maybe there's a worship center?" I began to pace, searching again. "Like a shrine or something?"

Cade joined me in my hunt. We searched the entire length of the wall, finally finding a large flat stone set into the side wall east of the fort. It'd been hidden behind the castle. The foundation of the wall showed an alcove built into it.

Excitement thrummed in my chest.

Cade looked at me, then stepped into the center of the stone.

Magic flared on the air, surging with a ferocity that almost made me stumble. The air swirled with sparking magic as the stones that made up the castle began to break away, returning to the foundations of the Roman fort.

"Holy fates," I murmured.

Light glowed around Cade as the stone blocks flew through the air. Soon, the castle was gone, and the foundations were complete. Wooden walls began to grow out of the foundation, the fort returning to how it had once been.

"Whoa." I spun in a circle, taking it all in.

The walls rose twenty feet into the air, platforms built at the top for defense. The Romans had been trying to hold on to their territory in England, and this fortress had clearly been one of their main garrisons.

"Look." Cade pointed toward the alcove where the foundations of the shrine had been located.

Now, it was a complete shrine. A large flat stone sat upright and contained a carving of Cocidius. Like the one we'd seen before, it was a simple inscription of a man holding a shield and sword.

Only this time... "It's glowing."

"It's the entrance."

Cade stepped off the center stone and waved me toward him, then held out a hand. I slipped my hand into his larger one.

He looked down at me. "Ready?"

I nodded. "Ready."

Mayhem appeared at my side.

"Hey there, looking for an adventure?" I asked.

She yipped.

"Glad to have you." I rubbed her ghostly head.

We walked toward the glowing carving of Cocidius. The stone was taller than we were, the carving nearly the size of Cade. He stepped toward it. The stone platform and spell had mistaken his godly power for that of Cocidius. Hopefully the portal would do the same.

One Celtic war god was as good as another, right?

I sure hoped so.

Cade stepped through the carved stone, and his foot disappeared into the rock.

"Whoa."

I followed him inside, Mayhem pressing close against me. Magic shivered coolly against my skin as the rock enveloped me. It felt more like mist than stone, though my heartbeat still ratcheted up as my face neared the rock.

I squeezed my eyes shut and lunged through, focusing on the warm grip of Cade's palm.

Cold mist touched my face, then disappeared.

I opened my eyes.

Large trees towered all around us. The fort was gone.

"Ancient Oaks," Cade said. "Long since cut down by the Royal Navy to build their ships."

"This is what England used to look like?"

He nodded. "A different land."

I turned, noting the magic that sparked on the air. It smelled vaguely of blood, like Cocidius's. The forest itself was shadowed, the trees cutting out the light. The ground was dark, almost black.

Despite it all, the place felt like Earth, not like a true godly realm. Not like Yggdrasil and the realm of the Norse gods that I'd visited.

"It feels like a mirror realm," Cade said. "Like we're actually walking upon the earth, but in another dimension."

"It's weird." The portal that we'd exited glowed gold. I was glad we had the heavenly transport stone and could get out of here in a jiffy if we needed to.

The sound of a horn broke through the silence of the forest.

I stiffened. Cade spun around, searching for the source of the sound. It came again. Then the baying of hounds. *Or wolves.*

Near my head, Mayhem growled low in her throat.

"War dogs," Cade said.

"Or hunting." My gaze caught on the portal again. It pulsed with golden light. "Could they have been alerted to our arrival? Could they be hunting *us*?"

The baying hounds sounded closer.

Mayhem growled again.

"Run," Cade said.

He took off through the forest. I followed, sprinting to keep up. He held himself back so he didn't leave me behind, and I wondered why he didn't shift. We'd be faster if he were in his wolf form.

Panting, I raced behind him, leaping over tree roots and dodging large rocks. The wind tore at my hair as my lungs burned.

The sound of the hounds and the horn broke through the loud heave of my breaths. Ahead of us, a wide, dark river gleamed with light.

"We'll cross," Cade said. "Make them lose our scent."

I called upon my magic from the Norse god Njord, commanding the river water to part. It split, rushing away from a thin trail of dry land that cut straight through the river.

We sprinted across the river rocks. As soon as we reached the dry land on the other side, I allowed the water to crash back into place, concealing our scent.

Cade sprinted toward higher ground, an area where a cliff rose tall at the edge of the forest. My chest ached as I ran behind him, Mayhem at my side.

Man I could really use a wolf ride right about now.

We reached the cliff, which was jagged with many large outcroppings. He began to climb, swift and sure. I followed, scrambling my way up the rock. The cliff face turned to the side, and he followed it until we were partially concealed behind some rocks.

We were high enough up that the dogs couldn't get us right away, and we could always run for it, continuing along the side of the cliff.

I leaned back against the stone, panting.

In the distance, the horn and dogs sounded. They were moving slowly closer.

I gasped. "I think they're definitely hunting us."

"Aye."

"Why didn't you shift into a wolf? We'd be faster."

"I don't want them to know who I am. My magic is distinct. In my wolf form, it's even more so."

"Smart." He was right. We didn't want to reveal our hand too soon.

The forest was quiet save for the distant sound of the hunters and our breaths.

"Do you think these are Cocidius's men?" I asked.

"I hope so. We need to find out. Perhaps we can follow them to their master."

"As long as they don't catch us." I didn't want to meet those war dogs face to face. Mayhem was more my style. She fluttered in the air next to me, panting. Then emitted a fiery little fart, and looked startled.

I stifled a laugh—now was *not* the time—and turned to Cade. "I'm going to use Loki's power to make myself invisible and fly over them to see if I can figure out who they are."

He looked torn, as if he didn't like me going alone, but finally, he nodded. "Be careful."

"You too. Stay here. I'll come back to find you."

He reached up, and his big hand cupped the back of my neck. Gently, he pulled me forward, pressing a kiss to my lips.

Heat flared, along with affection, and I returned the kiss, reluctantly pulling away after a moment.

"I find that saying goodbye to you becomes harder and harder," he said.

I leaned my forehead against his chest and murmured, "Same."

I swore I could feel his grin against the top of my head. Before I lost any will to move, I pulled away and let my wings unfurl from my back.

"That's more impressive every time I see it," he said.

I looked back at the silvery feathers, a little thrill of pleasure going through me. "Agreed."

"Be careful."

I nodded, pushing off into the air, my wings carrying me toward the tops of the huge oaks. I called on Loki's magic of illusion, imagining myself as invisible. The power shivered over me, letting me know it had worked. I turned back and looked down at Cade, who watched me from the cliff.

He shot me a thumbs-up.

Good. I was definitely invisible. I didn't want to be caught because my magic didn't work.

I whirled away from Cade and flew faster, high above the trees, following the baying of the hounds.

Wind whipped through my hair as I flew. The orange sun flared bright as it dipped toward the horizon, casting the forest below with shadow.

A bird flew past me, faltering as it neared. It was a small one —maybe a sparrow—and it turned its little head to look at me, bright eyes seeming confused.

Could it see me?

Eventually the bird flew on, and I ignored it, pushing myself toward the hunters.

They weren't far off. Maybe a few hundred yards from where

Cade stood. A flash of movement in the trees below caught my eye. I swooped low.

Bingo.

There were a dozen mounted hunters, all of them wearing strange-looking leather clothes—like the stuff you'd see on a museum dummy. Six hounds, giant scraggly things that looked almost like wolves, trotted nearby, noses glued to the ground for scent. They crossed the river and were trying to pick up our trail again.

Eventually they would find it.

I dipped lower, trying to figure out if they were associated with Cocidius in some way. I could already tell that he wasn't amongst their number—they had strong magic, but nothing like a god's.

And, even more tellingly, none of them had giant horns sheathed in gold.

One of the men turned his horse, showing me his back. The leather tunic that he wore was burned with a design—that of a simple figure holding a sword and shield.

Jackpot.

I was about to fly back to Cade when a bird cawed. Then another.

I glanced around.

A group of hawks flew toward me, little leather strips hanging from each of their right feet.

Their black gazes burned with intent—and all were pinned to me.

From below, the hounds bayed, louder than ever.

I glanced down.

Each dog looked up, eyes riveted to me.

Oh, crap.

Could they see me?

3

The warriors looked skyward, searching. Their heads turned and eyes darted. They couldn't see me.

But their animals could sense me. Only now did I notice the leather armbands they each wore—protection from their hawks.

I turned and darted away, pushing my wings to carry me far and fast. My heart thundered in my ears as the dogs barked louder and faster. A flash of black appeared in my vision.

A hawk!

It bombed, going for my wings. A sharp prick of pain flared in my left wing. The hawk had gouged me with its claws or beak.

I darted away, but another hawk met me, digging its sharp claws into my arm. It took everything I had not to cry out. Not to drop the illusion.

The birds attacked with ferocity, somehow sensing my presence. I veered away from the path back to Cade. I wasn't going to be able to outrun these creatures. I couldn't lead them—and the hunters—to Cade.

Pain flared all over my body as I tried to outfly the hawks. Wind tore at my hair. I occasionally dipped low enough that the tree branches clawed at my legs, but the hawks kept coming.

I drew my sword and shield from the ether. With a hiss of pain, I swung the shield toward an oncoming hawk. It slammed into the metal, then wheeled away. But another bird came after it. And another.

Mayhem shot from the forest below, flying right for a hawk. She shot a blast of fire toward it, singing the hawk's wings. The bird shrieked and spun away. But there were still a dozen of them.

Mayhem did her best, darting around in full attack mode, her dragon form flickering over her pugly one. She was able to keep some of the birds off me, but others darted past. They were too fast to hit with my sword, and they drove me lower, toward the ground.

"Go, Mayhem!" I didn't want her getting caught by the hunters.

They thundered along below, their horses' hooves a cacophony against the forest floor. The hounds bayed, bloodlust in the sound.

Panic thundered in my chest, my heart threatening to break my ribs. I panted, awkwardly trying to dodge tree limbs as the hawks drove me on.

I just needed to get up high again!

Except the hawks flew above me, keeping up their attack. More joined them.

So many!

Lungs and muscles burning, I was only fifteen feet above the ground when I caught sight of Cade running through the forest, headed for the hunters, who hadn't yet seen him.

Idiot!

He'd try to save me. And maybe he could go up against twelve hunters and six hounds—very possibly—but it was such a risk. And these hawks were so damned ferocious.

I extended my power of illusion to him, turning him invisible. But the hounds' baying faltered. They turned their heads toward him, nostrils quivering.

Damn!

They'd caught his scent. Just like the birds had caught mine. The dogs wheeled, darting toward him.

Pain flared at my scalp. A hawk dug its claws in. Agony shot through me. My wings faltered. The pain distracted me, and a branch struck my left wing. I lost control, tumbling through the air.

I skidded against the ground, rolling head over heels, until I slammed against a tree.

Panic flared in my chest as I struggled to rise. My wings made it hard, so I absorbed them back into my body.

My magic faltered, the illusion flickering due to the pain and exhaustion. Invisibility was the most difficult skill, and I was starting to lose my grip on it.

When a dog jumped on me and tore at my shoulder with his teeth, I felt the magic fall away completely. In the distance, Cade appeared as my invisibility magic fell away from him, too.

Shit!

I slammed my shield against the war dog, forcing the animal away, and threw an illusion toward Cade, imagining his bone structure changing slightly. If we were going to run into Cocidius, we didn't want him recognizing us. I used the last of my magic to give Cade lighter brown hair and heavier features. I did the same to myself, praying that it worked. They were small changes, enough for me to hold on to, but hopefully they'd do the job.

The dog came for me again, muzzle drawn back from its fangs. I raised my sword and shield, crouching low. More dogs prowled closer, and in the distance, the eight mounted riders approached. Four more hunters were off their horses, necks broken.

Cade's doing?

I swung my sword, making the attack dog back up and growl. As I held off the dog, I watched Cade leap for a fifth mounted hunter.

He'd nearly reached him when one of the men threw a silver rope toward him. It glinted as it flew through the air and wrapped around Cade, pinning his arms to his side.

He roared, face turning red as he strained to break the rope.

"Struggling will have no effect," one of the men shouted.

I shouldn't have been able to understand him—it was clear that his language was different—but somehow I could. Magic of the godly realm, perhaps.

Cade thrashed, but it did no good. A war dog plowed into his side, throwing him off his feet and to the ground.

The dogs that lunged for me suddenly quit their attack, darting away. I had only a moment to feel dread before silver glinted in the air.

A rope slammed into me, the ends wrapping around me like a terrible embrace. My arms pinned to my sides, I dropped my sword and shield, unable to maintain my grip.

Panic flared, my skin chilling.

I left my weapons where they lay. I didn't need to retrieve them, or even store them in the ether right now. The expensive magic that allowed me to use the ether as storage would retrieve them for me. And I didn't want to reveal to these hunters that I had that power.

A dog crashed into my side, sending me flying to the ground. Leaves lodged in my hair, and my cheek rubbed against the dirt. Overhead, hawks circled and cawed.

A man leaped down from his horse. I struggled as he stomped near, desperate to break my bonds.

In the distance, Cade was lifted by three men and tossed into the back of a small wagon that I hadn't noticed earlier. He was still bound in the magical rope. If he couldn't break through, neither could I.

I lay still, panting. The boots stopped in front of my face, and the man bent down and swung me up over his shoulder.

My stomach slammed into his shoulder and the breath whooshed out of me, pain flaring in my middle.

"Bastard," I muttered.

He chuckled, an ugly sound, and carried me to the wagon. He tossed me in next to Cade. I was aligned so that I could see the back of his head. We had both lost our backpacks in the fight.

Fortunately, I hadn't seen Mayhem in a while, which could only be a good thing.

"Yah!" shouted a man, and the cart began to move. It bounced slowly over the forest floor as the horse pulled it behind the warriors.

The dogs trotted along, sniffing us, their gazes bright with interest.

"So, this isn't ideal," I murmured.

Cade turned until he was facing me. No one was around, so I let the illusion fall away. He looked normal again, thank fates.

"At least we're headed straight for him," Cade murmured.

"I hope so." I recalled the symbol on the back of the man's tunic. It was our best hope—and if we were lucky, they lived in the same place as Cocidius.

"Let's see how this plays out," Cade murmured. "It could work in our favor."

I shifted against the tight binding, every inch of my body burning from the pain of the animal attacks. Blood slicked much of my skin, cooling in the night air. Darkness was falling, bringing with it a greater feeling of danger.

"I hope you're right," I murmured. "Because this feels pretty dire."

About thirty minutes later, after the sun had fully set and I'd used some of my magic to heal my wounds, I heard the sound of a town. Talking people and lowing cattle, along with the clang of metal and a low thudding noise.

"I think we're almost there," Cade murmured.

"Thank fates." It had been a miserable ride. I was freaked out about what we might face in town, but I was beyond ready to get out of the cart.

Nerves made my breath come short as golden light began to glow in the distance. I called upon my magic, giving Cade and myself the same simple glamour I'd done earlier. I didn't know if we'd see Cocidius, but just in case, I wanted to be prepared.

Fortunately, it was getting easier and easier to use Loki's magic. Which was good, since the last thing we needed was for Cocidius to recognize us. And I was tired, most of my power sapped.

For his part, Cade suppressed his magical signature, keeping it tightly controlled. He left the scent of a storm at sea so he didn't appear completely powerless—that would send alarm bells of its own since powerful supernaturals could conceal their magic. Better to try to run under the radar as nobodies. I did the same, having to work harder to conceal my new magic. It didn't come naturally to me. Hopefully the hunters hadn't noticed earlier.

The cart bounced toward the town. As it rolled past the first ancient round building, I caught sight of a wary looking man with a metal ring around his neck.

I frowned.

Yeah, that guy didn't want to be here.

Behind him, the round building was made of wood with a thatched roof.

"Iron Age," Cade murmured. "A common type of dwelling."

"It looks like Cocidius likes to live in the old style." We'd gone back in time. Sort of. I didn't know how.

"Or it's all that his realm can manage."

"More likely." We rolled past more simple round structures. Smoke curled up from the center of the conical roof, glowing orange in the light of dozens of flickering torches.

All around, people stared at us. Those with iron rings around their necks looked dead-eyed. The bigger, heartier individuals—nearly all male—barely spared us a glance.

They were the warriors—the elite in this realm of the warrior god.

"This isn't what your realm would look like, right?"

"If I had one?" Cade shook his head, which was a bit weird, since he looked different. "Hell no. I don't mind rustic so much. But all these people in chains? The warriors stomping around like they're the baddest jerks in the place? Not for me, thanks."

"That's what I figured." I took it all in, searching for an escape route—searching for Rowan.

I should've felt her, right?

I had to assume so.

She was my *sister*.

But I hadn't felt her before. I'd faced off against her—fighting to kill. *I'd almost killed Rowan.*

The thought made me shudder.

"You all right?" Cade murmured.

"Fine." But I couldn't help the gross nausea that pooled in my middle. I could have killed her and never realized.

But now I knew. And I could only hope that whatever curse they'd put on her, I could break it.

I just had to figure out what it was.

And find her.

I craned my neck to get a better look around, hoping to see

her despite the fact that I couldn't sense her here. It was really more of a war camp than a village. There were no families or children—just warriors and slaves. They were all either cleaning weapons, making weapons, or cooking.

Fighting and eating seemed to be all they did here. The dark night created a dome over the warmly lit camp, and it'd be cool to be witnessing history. If I weren't tied up in the back of a cart about to be fitted with a metal collar of my own.

The cart rolled to a stop in front of a rustic, covered pavilion. A large table was spread with scrolls and small wooden figurines.

My breath caught for a half second before I realized that Cocidius wasn't here.

"Where's Cocidius?" I whispered. This was definitely the headquarters of his war camp.

"I can't sense him here," Cade said. "But these are definitely his men."

A hulking bruiser of a guy stepped around the table. He was draped in rough leather, with a variety of wicked looking blades hanging from a wide belt. A scar sliced diagonally down the middle of his face. He'd nearly lost an eye, but had gotten lucky.

"Where did you find them?" His voice sounded like rocks grinding together.

"Edge of the eastern lands." The voice came from the front of the cart. "Not sure what they are. Not our normal haul."

The scarred man sniffed and spat, then kicked Cade's foot where it hung off the edge of the cart.

Anger flared in Cade's eyes. No doubt he could wipe the floor with the loser who was looking us over like prime cuts of beef. But that wouldn't help us find Cocidius.

Cade glanced at me. I briefly shook my head. He nodded, then lay still, a bored expression on his face.

"Well, toss them in with the others," the scarred man said.

"We'll see what they're made of in the morning. Good to have fresh meat."

Fresh meat?

I stifled a groan. I'd have happily gone all my life without being called fresh meat.

I made a mental note to punch this jerk if I got the chance. Apparently bad clichés were timeless. And the only fresh meat I wanted anything to do with came straight from the butcher.

The cart rolled away from the pavilion. We passed a fighting ring that looked like an old corral full of wounded men, all of them going at each other with a ferocity that belied the extent of their wounds. Next, we passed rows upon rows of tents. Then another fighting ring.

Finally, we stopped next to a large roundhouse. Two burly guards stood outside the door, their arms crossed over their chests and their faces set like cement. Their scowls didn't budge as one pulled open the door and the other approached the cart.

He grabbed my ankle and hauled me out, then carried me into the roundhouse and tossed me on the hard ground.

I crashed down, pain singing through me. Cade landed hard next to me.

The door slammed shut.

I blinked, trying to adjust to the dark.

A glow from overhead lit our surroundings. People leaned against the walls, all of them staring at us with disinterest. I struggled, trying to escape my bonds, but they didn't budge. More blank stares came our way.

"Well, this sucks," I muttered.

"Seconded," Cade said. "What a bastard."

A low chuckle sounded from behind us. I craned my neck to catch sight of the person who had laughed.

A skinny red-haired girl leaned against the wall, her arms crossed over her chest as she stared at us. She was about my age, maybe a bit younger, and her hair was done in a messy crown of braids. Her leather pants were worn, and her tunic had a tear in the sleeve. Dirt streaked her pale skin, and her eyes looked far older than her years.

She met my gaze, but didn't crack a smile, despite the previous chuckle.

But then, what was there to smile about?

I was as much a prisoner as she was.

Not that I'd be one for long. And there was no way in hell I'd be leaving these people behind either. I didn't know why they were locked up in here like livestock, but I knew they didn't deserve it.

I was going to save Rowan, and light this place up on the way out.

The girl glanced around, then sighed dramatically. "So it's my turn, is it?"

"It's always your turn," grumbled the man next to her. He looked about a decade older than her, his face wearier.

"Alllll right." She dusted off her palms and climbed to her feet, then strolled over to us.

I eyed her warily.

"Now, don't look at me like that," she said. "I'm not the one who trussed you up."

"Sorry," I said.

She reached toward my waist and grabbed the end of the enchanted rope, then pulled. It slipped away from me like it was nothing, and I hopped to my feet.

"Thanks." I reached down and pulled on Cade's rope. It came away easily.

She held up the rope and frowned at it. The rope no longer glinted silver and hung dull and limp.

"Piece of shit," she muttered. "The magic always goes as soon as it's used."

I thought it was clever, but I could see how she might be annoyed if she spent her time locked up here with nothing but the floor and some grumpy companions.

"What is this place?" I asked.

Her brows rose. "You don't know?"

I shook my head. "I mean, I have some ideas. But why are you locked up here?"

She chuckled, then strolled back to her spot on the wall. I glanced at Cade, who nodded. We followed her, and I sat next to her, leaning against the wood and inspecting my dismal surroundings.

She gestured to the room. "Now, you might think that I spend time here because I like it." She tilted her head toward me, a deadpan expression on her face. "But you'd be wrong."

"I can't say I'm surprised."

"Well, no. I imagine you are not." She leaned her head back against the wall. "You've been captured by the war god Cocidius —or his lackeys, at least."

A roar came from outside of the roundhouse, a cacophonous sound created by dozens of people. Maybe even hundreds.

"What's that?" I asked.

She smiled grimly. There was no joy on her face. "The reason you were abducted. Tomorrow, you'll be tossed in that fight ring to prove yourself."

My head whipped toward her. "What?"

Still leaning against the wall, she turned her head to look at me. "Never heard of Cocidius's fight ring?"

"No."

"Where are you from?"

"Um..." Did I say I was from the future? *Was* I from the future? Or was this currently the future, just totally old-school looking? Like, Iron Age old-school.

"Don't worry about it," she said. "I understand."

"So you don't say where you're from either?"

"Oh no, I have no problem with that. I'm Maira, from Pendock, little village at the edge of Cocidius's realm. That's where most of us are from—the outlying villages."

"So you're part of his godly realm?"

"Essentially, yes. Though we don't worship him." She scoffed. "Who would do that, I have no idea. Now, Belatucadros. That's a real war god."

I stiffened slightly, feeling Cade do the same where my arm was pressed against his. I glanced at her to see if she realized who she was sitting near.

She gave me a look that suggested I was stupid. "Belatucadros. You know of him, right?"

"Um, yes. I do."

"He's a real war god, right? Not some arse who kidnaps people and makes them fight in his fight rings."

"He definitely doesn't do that," Cade said from beside me. "Not his style."

I glanced at him. The glamour still concealed his true features, and he was suppressing his magic. If it helped to reveal himself, he would, I assumed.

Right now, we didn't know if it would.

"So Cocidius captured you for his fight ring?"

"Or to be a slave. But I'm mean and scrappy, so I get a shot at the ring."

"You say it like it's a good thing."

Her brows lowered. "I'd rather die fighting than wear a collar."

"Amen."

"Amen?"

Right. The ancient Celts probably didn't say *amen*. "It just means I agree. Have you been in the ring?"

She nearly growled. "No. Been here a week and I've been

stuck here. If I could win a fight, I might move to the training compound. Better accommodation. But I haven't gotten my shot yet, so I'm here. Waiting."

"Has anyone tried to escape?" Cade asked.

"Can't. The guards are too strong. Cocidius gave them some of his power. We wouldn't stand a chance."

"Do you have magic?" Normally, I'd assume yes. She knew about the ancient gods, who were real, and the magical rope.

"Some of us do. We use it in the ring. I'm a fire mage. What are you?"

I wasn't about to say DragonGod, so I went with water mage, which seemed to satisfy her. "So no one even tries to use their magic to escape?"

"Most of us don't have magic. Those who do.... Well, they manage us well. Some are in a special roundhouse where their magic is dampened. But not me. No need. I spend all my time in this wooden house. I can't exactly light it up. They'd let us burn in here. And if I ever get to the fight ring, the escort will be so heavy it'd be a death wish to fight back."

Bastards. I'd do something about this. No way I was leaving these people captive in here. But I'd have to take out the Rebel God to do it. "Have you seen Cocidius?"

She shook her head. "He shows up sometimes, I've heard."

Hopefully he'd come soon.

She smacked her knee. "Right. I'm going to lie down and go to sleep. Tomorrow might be my big day."

She stretched out on the floor, her hands crossed over her stomach. She looked almost content.

"How are you so happy?" I asked. She'd been locked up here a week. No doubt miserable and scared.

She slitted an eye open. "Things aren't bad yet. Maybe one day they'll get bad. Not today, though."

I nodded. I thought this was actually pretty bad, but there

was no need to say it. Whatever had made this girl so tough had to be a hell of a doozy.

I slouched down and leaned my head against Cade's shoulder. I whispered low enough that only he could hear. Almost everyone was lying down to sleep, anyway. "Was this what you were expecting?"

"I wasn't sure what to expect. But this doesn't surprise me."

"Me neither. What a bastard."

"I don't know what your plan is, but I'm thinking we play along for a little while. We could bust out of here now that the chain is off, but lying low is better. We'll fight in the ring, get the lay of the land. When Cocidius shows up, we steal your sister, kill him, and then blast this place to hell and set all the prisoners free."

I smiled against his shoulder. "You read my mind."

4

"Wake up!"

The roar dragged me from a fitful slumber against Cade's shoulder. I jerked upright, heart pounding.

Light streaming in through the door illuminated the round room. Groggy prisoners sat up, rubbing their eyes, and I suddenly remembered where I was.

Captive.

I shifted, the dried blood making my clothes stiff and my skin itchy. Next to me, Cade climbed to his feet, towering over me. I made sure that I used Loki's power to keep the glamour on our faces. Illusion was turning out to be handy.

"You!" The guard pointed at Cade. "Don't move!"

"Relax, man." Cade reached a hand down and I took it, letting him haul me to my feet.

After a night on the cold, hard floor, everything ached.

"I'm warning you!" The guard raised a spear.

Cade lifted his hands. "Just standing up, pal."

Maira, the red-haired girl, hopped to her feet next to us. "Don't worry about him. He's a right bastard, that one."

I gave the burly guard a quick up and down. "I can see that."

He stalked toward us, pointing his spear. "You two. The new ones. You're up first."

"Hey!" Maira said. "I've been waiting forever!"

The guard tried to backhand her, but she ducked, darting back toward the wall. The other prisoners snickered.

The guard's face turned red, and he roared, "Shut up, or you'll all be fed to the dogs."

I wrinkled my nose. A diet of humans couldn't be good for the dogs. Not to mention the humans.

The guard grabbed my arm and tugged me forward. Cade emitted a low growl.

I glanced back and gave him a *look*. "Chill out. It's fine."

The guard grabbed Cade's arm, too. He was Cade's size, but that didn't mean much. Cade looked down at the guard's hand as if he were looking at a fly.

He frowned, then looked up. "Let's go, then."

"You don't give the orders. I do," the guard snapped.

I grinned. As long as we weren't wrapped in that magic lasso, Cade would wipe the floor with this guy. But better to let him have his sense of power. Easier for us to do our job.

Cade seemed to agree, because he nodded his head and tried to look contrite.

A tiny laugh almost escaped me. Cade looked more constipated than contrite. I got the feeling *contrite* wasn't a thing he felt often, and he was a shit actor.

The guard hauled us from the room. I glanced back at Maira, who stared after us.

I'd get her out of here. No matter what it took. I'd get them all out.

The midmorning sun blazed as we stepped out into the little village. Most of the ground was pressed dirt, but some grass peaked up here and there. Clusters of roundhouses were surrounded by tents, and horses stamped in a corral nearby.

"Any chance we're going to breakfast?" I asked the guard. "Maybe a bath?"

He barked a laugh. "First, you fight. If you don't die, then you eat." He looked me up and down, his nose wrinkled in disgust. "Maybe they'll throw you in the river after."

I itched so badly from the dried blood that I actually wouldn't mind.

He hauled us toward the edge of town. Most of the people we passed wore ragged cloth and leather, accented by a collar around their necks. Bile rose in my throat.

I sucked in a ragged breath and focused on the task at hand. We had to take out Cocidius if we were going to free these people.

"What are we fighting?" Cade asked.

"Depends on the Ring Master's preference," the man said.

Great. The Ring Master sounded like a freakin' delight.

The guard dragged us up toward a strange-looking arena. The fight ring within was the size of a football field and roughly oval with massive stone platforms all around. They were at least twenty feet tall, forming a wall that would trap the fighters within. Warriors sat on the platforms, decked in leather armor and weapons, and cheered and raised their fists.

In the middle of the dirt arena, a man fought a huge, horned demon. Each was armed with a blade, but the man also seemed to be throwing out some kind of small sonic boom that drove the demon backward.

A bite of pain struck me, longing for my lost magic.

I sucked in a breath and used the pain to focus my will. I had to control my magic—show them only what I wanted them to see.

A water mage. That was all I was. No more, no less.

And certainly not a winged Valkyrie, the Dragon God of the Vikings. No siree.

"This way." The guard pushed us into a smaller corral pressed up against the side of the fight ring. A gate led into the ring, and a burly man leaned against it, scowling as he watched the fight within.

Several people sat on benches along the sides—fighters, I thought. A few guards stood at the ready, their hands gripped lightly around their sword hilts.

"Got you the two new ones, Cedric." Our guard shoved us toward the man who watched the fight.

He turned, looking us over. He wore leather armor and had long, straggly hair. His gaze was cunning, though, and I stiffened my spine, trying to control my magical signature and not give too much away.

Cade controlled his magic perfectly—I got almost nothing off of him—and he slouched his shoulders and glared.

He was trying to go for less threatening, but it didn't really work. A god trying to hide amongst normal supernaturals was always a tough sell.

"Are you the Ring Master?" I asked.

"Trainer," he grunted. He sniffed the air. Trying to get a hit of my magic.

His gaze met mine. "Water mage?"

"Yep." *No more, no less.*

His gaze turned to Cade. His brow wrinkled as if he had a hard time placing him. "Healer," he finally said. "But what else?"

"Gladiator," Cade said.

Smart. He was no gladiator, but claiming the species was smart. Gladiators were a type of supernatural who were descended from the original Roman warriors. They were strong and fast—two skills that Cade had in spades.

The trainer nodded. "You fight next. Do well, you'll be rewarded."

"What are we fighting?" I asked.

"I don't know. But you'll go in together."

That was good. I preferred it that way. Teamwork was better every time.

A flash of energy hit me—an awareness. I gasped.

My sister was here.

I could feel her.

Vibrating, I turned toward the arena. Searching. Searching.

There were warriors and fighters and slaves.

But no Rowan.

No Cocidius, either.

"Where is Cocidius?" I asked, not wanting to mention my true interest.

"He doesn't attend the preliminary fights." The trainer turned toward the fight, leaning his arms on the railing.

Dang.

So I had to survive this, get some rewards, like he'd said, and level up to the next round. Then I could fight in front of Cocidius. My fists clenched. I couldn't wait to get ahold of that abducting bastard.

Cade reached for my hand and squeezed. I leaned slightly into him, appreciating the gesture. It gave me strength. Patience.

I needed a lot of patience, considering that Cade and I could bust right out of here if we wanted. But that would alert Cocidius, and we couldn't risk that.

The fighter in the ring finally got lucky and landed a blow, plunging his blade through the heart of the demon. The monster roared and flailed, falling backward.

The victor shouted, raising his arms and bloody sword in victory, then stomped toward us.

The trainer opened the gate, and the man charged through. As soon as he'd passed, the trainer gave Cade a shove.

Cade stiffened, clearly not used to being bossed around, then strode into the ring. I followed, heart pounding as the roar of the crowd rushed over me. Their bloodthirsty gazes burned.

I stepped up next to Cade, glancing at him. "I can't figure out if this sucks or if it's is going to be fun."

He chuckled. "Maybe a bit of both. But use minimal magic."

That definitely meant no wings, then. Still... "Let's give them a show."

To the right, a man in a long white cape stepped up onto the front of a rock. I blinked at the brightness of his garb, realizing that everyone in this realm wore some shade of beige or brown. Up till now, the only color was green.

Yep. He was the Ring Master.

The man raised his arms, magic sparking around his hands.

The crowd roared louder, their faces red.

The man lowered his arms, and the crowd silenced. His voice boomed out over the arena. "The first to reach the other side of the arena wins a boon! You must jump through your own rings to qualify."

I glanced at Cade, whose brow was creased.

"He wants us to compete," I said.

"Fat bloody chance."

From across the arena about a hundred yards away, flames burst to life. Two sections of flame broke away from the main body of fire, shooting toward us.

"Go!" The trainer shouted from behind us.

The rings were flying toward us, large enough to jump through.

They were literally making us jump through hoops to complete this task.

I sighed and glanced at Cade, who nodded. We started running, each of us headed for our ring. The circle of flame moved incredibly fast and was on me within a few steps. It hovered two feet off the ground and was about six feet tall.

I leapt through without issue.

Cade, who was taller, had to pull some kind of weird ducking leap, but he made it fine.

Another flew at us, this one a little higher, and I leapt through, barely making it. Then the rings came faster and faster, some going left, then right. I darted across the arena like I was in a weird video game.

Soon, my lungs were burning and my skin was singed where the flame had hit me. Not all the rings were wide. Some, I could barely fit through.

Sweat rolled down my temples as the crowd roared. I was going as fast as I could, and Cade could have left me in the dust ages ago, but he stuck at my side, jumping through his own hoops with ease.

I passed the Ring Master, who was positioned roughly at the midpoint of the arena. He looked frustrated. By Cade holding back?

Because I was looking at the Ring Master, I nearly missed the flaming hoop that flew right at me. I leapt, muscles aching, and barely managed to clear the bottom of the hoop.

Were they getting higher?

The next caught my foot as I jumped, and I sprawled in the dirt.

Shit.

I scrambled up before Cade could dart over to help me, but he paused, waiting.

We were nearly to the end. If we could just make it...

The next ring that flew toward me was so damned tall I didn't stand a chance in the world.

Double shit.

Cade ran toward me so fast I hardly saw him. He knelt before the ring, holding out his cupped hands, and I took the hint, sprinting toward him full speed and then stepping high.

He vaulted me up, and I flew through the air, the hoop's flame singing me. As I sailed to the ground on the other side, I saw Cade race back to his own ring and jump through just in time, using his immense speed and strength.

Ha! Try to make us work against each other, my ass.

I sprinted toward the end of the arena, pulling to a panting stop in front of the wall of flame. Cade finished at the exact same time, considerably less winded. He looked like he'd had a nice jog, his hair nicely ruffled.

The flames died down, and I turned back to face the arena and the Ring Master. He raised his arms again, cape flapping in the wind.

I tried to catch my breath and waited for the next challenge.

"You must reach the other end of the arena. The first one wins their freedom!"

I glanced at Cade. "He's upped the ante."

"Or so he thinks."

"Doesn't know we're perfectly content being captives for the moment."

On the other side of the arena, a wave of blue water rose up, surging toward us. It was forty feet tall and roiling with white surf.

The first challenge had given Cade the advantage.

This one was mine.

I reached for Cade's hand. His strong grip closed around my own.

"Let's go." I sprinted toward the wave, Cade at my side.

As the huge wall of water crashed toward us, I peeked at the Ring Master out of the corner of my eye. Frustration seethed on his face.

As the wave neared us, I called on my gift of water.

We plunged into the liquid—intentional on my part, since I needed a bath—and then I forced the water away from us, forming an air pocket on the bottom of the wave. We never even lost our footing.

Cade and I ran through the blue wonderland, trapped in our own little bubble of air that moved with us. The mud underfoot stuck to my boots, and I sprinted faster.

Magic pressed in on me, an intense force that crushed my muscles.

The Ring Master was pitting his power against my own, trying to win control of the wave and drown us.

"You feel that?" Cade grunted.

"Do I ever." It was damned uncomfortable. "But he doesn't know who he's up against."

"A god."

"Sorta." I threw my magic outward, forcing the water away from us.

The Ring Master's magic weakened, almost snapping. I'd nearly overpowered his control!

Shit.

That wasn't good.

Look before you leap.

I didn't want to go too intense and reveal the extent of my strength.

"Pull back," Cade said.

"I know." I loosened my grip on the magic, not forcing the water as hard, and it flowed back toward us, decreasing the size of our bubble until there almost wasn't enough space to run without my knees splashing into the wave.

It took everything I had to manage the perfect amount of power that would keep us from drowning without igniting the Ring Master's suspicion.

By the time we reached the other side, I was panting and sweating.

We stumbled to a halt near the stone arena wall, and the water crashed away. I struggled to catch my breath.

"Well done," Cade murmured. "You've never controlled your magic so well."

"Practice makes perfect." And it wasn't controlling the water that was hard. It was making sure my godly powers didn't go haywire and fix every problem with a sledgehammer.

I turned around to face the Ring Master, who was staring at us with fiery eyes. Apparently his audience liked competition, and we weren't giving it to him.

"You will fight each other!" he roared.

"Nah," I shouted.

Cade chuckled.

From all sides of the arena, spears appeared. They floated on the air, pointing inward, their wicked points glinting in the morning sun.

"Seriously?" I muttered.

The spears pressed inward. The ones closest to us poked at my back, and I hurried forward. Cade followed, strolling leisurely across the ground. These weren't easy challenges, but the god of war was always confident.

Weapons appeared on the ground in front of us. Two swords and two shields.

"I suppose we could pretend to fight," I said. "I could throw myself onto the ground and pretend to be wounded."

"They won't buy it if there's no blood."

"Yeah, they look bloodthirsty."

The spears pressed us farther in, decreasing the size of our ring substantially.

I ignored the weapon on the ground. "We really aren't going to fight each other!"

"One must defeat the other in the trials!" the Ring Master shouted. "Then one shall pass through."

"Still not going to happen," Cade yelled.

The Ring Master yanked his raised arms down. The spears disappeared. "Then you will fight the Grallag!"

The crowd roared, the most bloodthirsty and excited sound I'd ever heard.

"Uh-oh," I said. "I bet the Grallag is super bad."

Black clouds of smoke began to waft up from the arena floor. It stank of sulfur and death. The black cloud rose high into the air, blocking out the direct light of the sun.

As the smoke slowly billowed toward us, I trotted over to the swords that were on the ground, deciding not to call my own from the ether. Best to keep that skill a secret.

I grabbed a sword and shield. Next to me, Cade grabbed another set.

Heart pounding, I turned to face the dark smoke. We might be prisoners of our own will, but the power radiating from the smoke made even me nervous.

"Keep close," Cade said. "Something big is coming."

Boy, was he right. The strength of the dark magic made my stomach turn. It absolutely reeked.

In a rush, the smoke flew away on the wind. In its place, a massive black monster loomed. The thing looked like a giant land octopus made of slimy, dark gray skin. A great mouth gaped open, fangs glinting in the sunlight.

I tried to count the legs, but there were so many. Far more than eight. They curled up into the sky, whipping in the air.

Oh, shit.

We'd been in control before this. Nothing we couldn't handle.

But I was pretty damned sure we couldn't handle a Grallag. It was the biggest monster I'd ever seen.

My heart thundered, fear chilling my skin.

"Ever seen one of these before?" I inched toward it, sword raised and heart thundering.

"Only heard of them. It's not a real animal. Just dark magic."

"Scary dark magic."

Cade frowned. "Aye. And there's something I can't remember about them. Tip of my tongue."

"Well, crap."

"Aye."

"Go for the legs, I assume?"

"They're its greatest weapon, so aye. Go for the legs."

"On it." I sprinted toward the monster, sword raised.

The crowd roared, voices deafening.

My head buzzed with fear.

The first tentacle whipped down toward me, so big and so fast that I couldn't get my sword up in time. I dived, rolling to the side and avoiding the slam of the tentacle by a hair's breadth.

I leapt to my feet and spun. As the octopus retracted its tentacle, raising it back toward the air, I sliced down with my blade, severing the limb.

The end of the tentacle flopped to the ground, black smoke billowing out. The stench made my eyes water. But at least the tentacle withered to dust.

"That's the way!" Cade shouted as he severed another tentacle, diving aside to avoid being blasted by the smelly air.

I sprinted around the Grallag's tentacles, darting and diving as they tried to smash me into the ground. I severed three, my head swimming with the stench of dark magic. Cade was even faster, using his godly speed to slice off many more.

High overhead, the Grallag hissed, a sound that sent shivers down my spine. I dared a glance upward, catching sight of its gleaming onyx eyes.

I froze dead, staring.

So beautiful.

So terrifying.

I shook my head, or tried to. But my head wouldn't move. No! I needed to look away.

But the monster's gaze had me snared.

I strained, trying to pull away. But I couldn't. Tentacles neared me.

"Move!" Cade shouted.

I tried to cry out that I couldn't, but my mouth wouldn't open.

Oh shit. Was this what Cade hadn't remembered? The Grallag had a stare that would freeze you if you met its gaze.

Yep.

The tentacle wrapped around my waist, squeezing tight. I gasped, struggling. But I couldn't move. No matter how I strained my muscles, none of them did a thing.

The Grallag looked away, no doubt searching for Cade.

Suddenly, my straining muscles jolted into action. I struggled in the Grallag's grip as it raised me high into the air, kicking and clawing and trying to stab with my sword.

Another tentacle knocked the sword from my grip.

"Bastard!" I searched for Cade, my ribs aching.

He raced around the Grallag, removing limbs with deadly efficiency. But there were so many.

One snuck around from behind him.

"Cade! From behind!"

He whirled, but it was too late. The tentacle wrapped around his waist, yanking him high into the air. He leaned over and swiped at the limb with a mighty strike of his sword.

It severed the tentacle, and he plummeted toward the ground.

I cheered.

But then another tentacle swooped in from below, pulling him up. A third tentacle yanked the sword from his grip.

Damn it!

The ground receded farther as the Grallag lifted me high. I thrashed, trying to break free, keeping my gaze riveted to Cade.

He struggled, his face turning red, but was unable to break the Grallag's grip.

For the first time, real fear spiking. Acid sliced through my veins, and my skin chilled. When the Grallag began to raise Cade high into the air and opened its mouth, I screamed.

It was going to eat us.

Holy fates, this giant hell octopus was going to eat us.

Terror and power welled inside of me.

Now was not the time to play it cool. We needed all the power we could get.

But water and healing and illusion wouldn't do me any good as long as the Grallag had me in its grip. And Cade might be able to shift, but he couldn't break the monster's grip.

Panic rose in my chest, my mind buzzing.

Clouds rolled overhead, thunder cracking in the air. Cold wind whipped by me as the atmosphere changed. Lightning struck high in the sky, a brilliant flash of gold.

I swore I could feel the electricity of it crackle through me.

Use it.

I gasped, eyes darting upward.

Lightning struck again. In my chest, I felt it, sparking with life.

Use it.

Holy freaking Thor. I'd felt this before. I was getting a new power.

Lightning.

From Thor.

I raised my hand to the sky, reaching for the lightning. Envisioning it in my mind and the energy shot through me. It smelled of ozone and felt like sparks.

The Grallag raised Cade directly over its mouth, maw gaping wide and fangs glinting in the light. He was just about to drop Cade inside—a crunchy god snack.

I called upon the lightning, imagining it striking down from the sky, strong and fierce. The power cracked through me, energy rising in my chest.

There was a risk that the lightning would flow through the Grallag and zap us too, but the gods wouldn't tell me to use it if that were the case, right?

I had no other options, and Cade was about to get it.

I reached for the lightning, desperation fueling me.

A massive bolt shot from the sky, plunging down toward the Grallag and striking it right in the head. The beast disappeared in a poof of smoke, a massive billowing cloud that rose up around me as I plummeted through the air.

I slammed into the ground, pain streaking through my leg. Residual lightning shock raced through my muscles, making them clench with pain. Had the Grallag been flesh and blood rather than magic, we might have died from the shock as it traveled from him into us.

I cried out, nausea welling up inside me. Tears stung my eyes as I leaned over and grabbed my leg. The pain shot harder.

"Ow!" Bad idea. My muscles twitched from the lightning shock, but at least we weren't dead.

"Bree!" Cade's voice came through the smoke.

I looked up. He limped through the dark fog, his arm wrapped around his chest. Broken ribs from the Grallag? My own hurt like the devil, too.

He knelt by my side. "Are you all right?"

"Yeah." I gasped, pain streaking through me. "Just a sprained ankle. Broken maybe."

"Rise!" The Ring Master's voice rang through the air.

The smoke had dissipated mostly, and I squinted through it, finally catching sight of his white cloak.

Cade reached down and hauled me to my feet.

I stood and doubled over with pain. "I really hope that was the last challenge."

"It was a close one." He gave me a knowing look, but didn't mention my new power.

"You are both victorious," the Ring Master shouted. He sounded a bit peeved, actually. "Go now!"

I didn't need to be told twice.

We both limped toward the exit. Cade kept me upright, but my ankle ached with every step. He made a move to pick me up.

"Don't even think about it," I muttered.

He grinned.

"But thanks." I just had to look strong. No way I'd get carried out of here.

I was sweating with pain by the time we reached the corral of fighters. Cade was pale, too.

"Internal injuries?" I murmured.

"I think so."

The trainer opened the gate, his gaze running up and down our bodies. "Go toward the left. The guard will take you to the healer."

"Then breakfast?" I'd already gotten my bath, but I didn't want to miss food.

"Yes."

"Good."

We limped toward the corral exit, where a burly man glowered at us before leading us toward the roundhouse with the healer. I'd prefer to heal myself, but didn't want to let that power slip.

"In here." The guard pushed open the door.

We entered a round, smoky room that smelled like sickness and death.

"Ew," I muttered.

"On the bench," the guard growled.

We took the nearest bench. A figure with a crazy nest of long gray hair and a stained robe worked in the corner, stirring a bubbling cauldron of something that smelled like old garbage and gasoline.

"Thank fates this isn't the breakfast stop," I said.

Cade chuckled.

"I'll be with you in a moment!" The healer cackled.

My gaze darted around, taking in the bloody tools and bowls and a tank full of worms.

I swallowed hard and leaned toward Cade. "I don't think we want this woman to heal us."

"Agreed."

I glanced toward the door where the guard had stood, but he'd stepped outside and closed it behind him. I couldn't blame him.

Yeah, whatever this healer wanted to do to us, I wanted no part of it.

"Heal yourself," I murmured.

Quickly, we went to work, using our magic to heal our wounds. Relief flowed through me as the pain faded, but exhaustion came on its heels.

I was nearly out of magic. Frighteningly so.

I'd need to recover.

We sat for ages as she stirred the cauldron. I wanted to leave, but we needed to pretend she'd helped us, or they'd figure out we had healing powers.

At least an hour passed before she turned, her dirty hair like a helmet around her head. She approached, and I realized that she wasn't the gray-haired old hag that I'd thought.

Nope.

She was just freaking filthy.

Her hair was actually blond, but it was coated in dust and ash. Dirt coated her face, and her eyes glittered with malice. Her magic stank of rotten garbage.

"What ails you?" she croaked.

A rat climbed out of her nest of hair, perching on her head like a silent sentinel, watching me with shining dark eyes. My gaze darted to him.

"Don't mind Boris." She pointed to her head. "He's my assistant. Very talented."

Boris hissed at me.

I looked away. Clearly that rat did not like eye contact.

But at least his hygiene was better than the healer's.

"Well, what's wrong with you?" she demanded.

Boris hissed again, seemingly for emphasis.

"Is that all he does?" I asked.

"It's very helpful."

Boris shot me the hairy eyeball.

"All right, all right, Boris." I held up my hands. "You're the foundation of this operation."

"I wouldn't go that far," the healer said.

But Boris preened, looking quite pleased. All right, the way to that rat's heart was through flattery. I had no problem flattering a rat if it got me what I wanted.

And right now, I wanted to be out of here.

I stood, holding out my arms. "Looks like I'm good as new. No more pain." I saluted the rat. "Thanks, Boris."

Cade stood as well. "I'm also fine." He nodded to Boris. "Thank you, sir, for healing us."

The rat bowed his head, whiskers twitching.

The witch healer sputtered. "But...but...!"

I hopped up and down. "See, no pain! So we'll be going now."

I turned, the image of Boris and the healer burned into my mind, and stepped outside. Cade followed.

I heard the woman sputtering behind me, and Boris squeaking.

"This way." The surly guard led us to the next roundhouse, which was absolutely massive.

"Is *this* breakfast?" I asked.

He just grunted, and pushed open the door. Cade entered first, and I followed. Though it was dimly lit, there was enough light to make out the long tables crowded with people. The scent of roasted meat made my mouth water.

"Finally."

"Hey!" a feminine voice shouted.

My gaze darted over.

Maira sat at a table, waving at us. She grinned wide, a black eye blooming in virulent shades of purple and blue.

"It looks like we have a friend," Cade said.

"Good. I'd hate to be the kid who sits alone at the lunch table."

"This isn't quite high school."

"No, that would be worse." At least from what I'd seen in the movies. Ana and I had been driving missions across Death Valley when we should have been in high school.

I hurried toward Maira, pleased when no one stopped me. It was nice to have freedom of movement, even if it was in this one building.

There were two spots on the bench across from Maira. On either side of her sat burly men who were plowing into hunks of meat. Their braids were dirty and ragged, but their teeth were strong as they went at the meat like wolves.

"You made it!" Maira said. "They've been telling me about

how you both made it through your challenge. Really angered the Ring Master, I heard."

"We did." I looked around. "But how did you get here? Last I saw, you were still in the captive's house."

"We're still captives, technically," the man next to her grunted.

"True." I reached for the large platter of meat and grabbed a piece. Cade was already digging in.

"I was called right after you," Maira said. "I fought the fight after yours. But it was quick, and I didn't have to go to the healer. I've heard she makes you wait ages."

"Sadistic bitch," the other man growled, meat juice glistening on his lips.

I looked away, grossed out, and took a bite of my own meat. I had no idea what it was, but it was tasty. In the corner, a flash of ghostly blue caught my eye. I turned, catching sight of Mayhem stealing a hunk of meat from a table.

No one seemed to notice her, but I grinned, pleased she was here. Lying low, but not so low she wouldn't steal a snack.

"I'm glad you made it out all right," I said.

"I knew I would." She held up the meat in her hand. "This isn't quite the feast I'd hoped for, but it will do. I'm just glad you two survived. They wanted to pit you against each other. Hard for two people to live through a fight to the death."

"True," Cade said.

I tore into the meat, realizing that it wasn't as good as I'd thought. I ate anyway, needing my strength.

"What happens now?" I asked.

"We get shown to our quarters," Maira said. "Depending on how well you did, you might get a better place to sleep. Then we fight tomorrow."

"Will Cocidius watch those fights?" I asked.

"Probably," she said. "He likes the big ones."

"Only goes to the best." The man at her left held out his hand. "I'm Aodh."

I shook his hand. "Hi, Aodh."

The other guy ignored us, so I ignored him.

"Is Cocidius here?"

"What are you, a god fucker?" Aodh asked.

Cade growled. I put a hand on his leg. He shut up, but didn't look happy about it.

"Not usually, no," I said. "But I can't help but be interested. Never saw a real god before."

"He's a bastard," Aodh muttered.

"Yeah, well, he threw me in a ring and made me fight a giant octopus made of black magic, so I can't help but agree."

Cade chuckled.

"He returned to camp a while ago," Maira said. "With some woman. Then they left. Went hunting or something."

Rowan. I'd felt her. Then her presence had disappeared.

"I heard they'll be back tomorrow," Aodh said. "For the fight."

Good. I wanted to ask more—like where he stayed when he was here and all that—but I didn't trust Aodh not to reveal my interest to the wrong person. And definitely not the silent guy on the other side of Maira.

So I zipped my lip and kept eating.

5

After the meal, guards led Cade and me to a small roundhouse toward the edge of the village. Another guard stood at the door, but he stepped back to let us enter.

Inside, there was a warm fire and a pile of furs on a straw mattress, along with some clean clothes.

I turned back to the guard who'd escorted us. "It's just us in here."

He nodded. "Korg will guard the door. Do not try to leave."

I held up my hands. "You don't have to worry about that."

He nodded, his gaze suspicious, and turned to leave.

I glanced at Cade. "I guess any time someone says not to worry about something, that's what you immediately start worrying about."

"Aye." Cade walked to the door, flipping a small wooden lock. It wouldn't keep people out if they really wanted to get in. One swift kick would do it. But it afforded a tiny bit of privacy.

I dropped the glamour that kept our true natures hidden.

Cade turned back to me, finally showing his real face.

It looked so much better.

"Why'd they give us such a good place?" I asked.

"I'd bet it's because hierarchies amongst prisoners sows discontent. We're less likely to join up and revolt if there is infighting. Especially if the strongest ones, the leaders, are separated from the masses."

"Smart." I sat on the mattress near the fire, warming my hands.

"Cocidius is nothing if he's not smart. He's risen a long way as a minor god."

"Minor god, major asshole."

While he paced around the small room, searching the walls for weakness, I stripped off most of my clothes, leaving myself in nothing but a bra and underwear. Quickly, I slipped under the blankets.

"Mind if I join you?" Cade asked.

It was the only bed in the room, so I raised the blanket. "I'd be delighted."

His gaze dropped, and I realized that he could see my bare stomach. Heat flushed through me.

I'd been so preoccupied with the danger of this that I hadn't realized what this was.

We were in a room, alone.

I was almost naked.

Now was not the time.

Not that it kept me from wanting him.

Heat raced through me as he stripped off his shirt. His skin gleamed in the firelight, the curves of his muscles highlighted by the flame. He was built like a god. Literally.

Cade toed off his boots and socks, then hooked his thumbs in his jeans. "Mind if I take these off? I've got underwear on."

I swallowed hard. "Not at all." I winced at the squeak in my voice.

Smooth, Bree. Real smooth.

He pushed his jeans down, revealing black boxer briefs and strongly muscled thighs.

Liquid heat raced through me.

He climbed into the bed next to me, his presence immediately warming me to my bones. I turned toward him, my gaze traveling from his heavily muscled chest up to his eyes. He watched me with enough intensity to make my blood warm.

"Hey." His voice was rough.

"Hey." Tension thrummed in the air between us, a living thing. It crackled and pulsed. Every breath that he took raised his chest, and I felt like I could feel it against my own despite the inches that separated us.

I itched to roll closer to him—to press my body to his and feel every inch of his strength. My mind raced with images of us together, making me shiver.

Unable to help myself, I leaned toward him, pressing a kiss to his lips.

Pleasure burst through me.

His big hands came up to grip my waist. They were warm and strong. I moved toward him. He pulled me closer until my chest pressed firmly against his.

The rich scent of him made my head swim. The smoothness of his skin cloaking the strength of his muscles was a drug.

"We should take it slow," he murmured against my lips. "Not lose our heads."

"I think I've already lost mine."

"Just a kiss."

"A few kisses." I pressed my lips to his. "Maybe a bit more."

He groaned and pressed a kiss to my lips, and I fell into it, losing whatever sanity I had left.

∿

The next morning, we woke before the guards came. We hadn't had sex last night—like Cade had said, now was not the time to lose our heads. The mission was too important.

And I really didn't want our first time to be interrupted by a surly guard who wanted to throw me into a fight ring. But we'd kept ourselves entertained, and memories of last night made heat rise inside me as I dressed.

Cade finished stoking the fire and turned. He'd redressed in his old clothes, as I had, ignoring the ones laid out for us. Our clothes might be dirty, but it felt better to wear our own stuff.

I met his gaze, then blushed.

Then I felt embarrassed, because I should be worldly enough not to blush.

Ah well, whatever.

He joined me on the low wooden bench by the fire. "So, what's our plan when we get out of here?"

"You're asking me?"

He shrugged. "I have some ideas, but this is your sister we're talking about. You get priority."

"Thanks." I leaned toward the flame and stared into it. "Mostly, we'll have to play it by ear. If we can find Maira and get some info, great. Ideally, we'd figure out where Rowan sleeps and steal her from there when it's quiet. Then we'll get her out of here using the heavenly transport charm. But before we leave for good, we help free the slaves."

"You get Rowan out of here. I'll lead the revolt."

I hesitated, wanting to stay behind to fight.

But Rowan. I had to put her first. I nodded. "And hopefully Mayhem will show up to help."

"I have no doubt that when you need her, she'll appear."

A loud banging sounded at the door.

My heart leapt into my chest, and I called upon Loki's magic, giving Cade and me the familiar glamour that was our disguise here.

The door crashed open, splintering the tiny lock.

Yep. I was super glad we hadn't had sex last night. Having this burly dude bust in on us would put me off the stuff for good.

He scowled down at us, his squished face looking like he'd taken too many rocks to the mug. "Time to fight."

I stood, brushing my hands off on my pants. "Lead on."

We followed him out the door. As soon as I stepped outside, he grabbed my arm, gripping tightly. I wanted to tell him not to worry about it—I wasn't running until I got what I came for—but that wasn't a great idea. The guard grabbed Cade's arm as well.

Cade looked down at his hand balefully, then back up at the guard. He sighed lightly, then nodded.

It was like a little old lady with a giant Great Dane pulling it on a leash. The only reason the old lady didn't go flying down the street was because the Great Dane didn't mind wearing the leash.

As the guard dragged us through the settlement, I took in as much as I could. There were still slaves wearing the collars, and they seemed to have free roam, within reason. None of the ring fighters were like us, though. They must've been kept on lockdown. But soldiers were everywhere.

These guys would be a problem when it came time to escape. But Cade could handle it.

The guard shoved us toward the waiting corral where I'd met the trainer yesterday. He didn't turn to look at us today, just hiked a thumb over his shoulder toward the benches at the back. The guard pushed us toward them, letting go of our arms.

I caught sight of Maira on the bench and grinned. Perfect. Just what I'd hoped for.

I snagged a seat next to her—the only one—while Cade

leaned against the back wall of the enclosure, arms crossed over his chest and eyes scanning the guards who wore armor and swords. There were at least ten of them in the waiting ring.

I leaned toward Maira, who grinned at me, and whispered, "How's it going?"

"Fine. I hear I'm going up against some ghouls."

I shuddered. "Don't let them scratch you."

She nodded. "Last thing I want is to turn into a ghoul."

"So what's the deal here? Why do some of the prisoners wear collars, and others don't?" The collars were going to be an issue, I could tell.

Her gaze darted around, checking to make sure no one watched us, and she leaned toward me slightly to whisper, trying to look casual. "Servant slaves wear the collars. Gives them free roam to do their jobs, but the magic prevents them from straying away from camp."

"Why don't fighters wear them?"

"Not enough, from what I heard. Valuable magic fuels the collars. There is a central source that powers them, but I don't know where it is. Fighters are just kept locked up like dogs and monitored pretty much every second of every day."

I nodded. "So you're locked in at night like us?"

"Yes. In a huge roundhouse at the edge of town. Shoved in like cattle."

"Then why did we get our own little place?" I asked.

She looked at me like I was stupid. "You can't have the powerful ones milling with the rest. You're the type of person with the skill to lead an uprising."

I nodded. Just like Cade has said. "Would you ever think of revolting?"

Her eyes widened, then narrowed with interest. She glanced around to make sure the coast was clear, then nodded slightly. "But how? We have no way to organize a revolt. No way to get weapons. The slaves with collars can't leave. And who would kill Cocidius? Only a god can kill another god."

"I've got some good news for you."

She leaned in.

My gaze traced over her face, searching for trustworthiness. I was putting a lot of faith in her now. She could blow this for us.

But I trusted her. Damned if I didn't. She reminded me of Ana. "Cade is Belatucadros. He's strong enough to take out Cocidius. And I'm a DragonGod. Strong enough to fight the soldiers and get you the weapons you need."

She inhaled sharply. "Are you serious? I couldn't feel his magic."

"He's got it locked up. So do I. We're good at controlling our signatures."

She nodded slowly, processing. "If that's true, you could leave here any time. You're too strong for them to contain. Why are you here?"

"Cocidius has my sister. We're here to save her. But I don't want to leave you or the others here. This is bullshit."

"That it is." She jerked her head decisively. "Okay, I'm in. What do we do?"

"I need some more info. Like where Cocidius sleeps, where's the armory, and what's the central source of the magic that enchants the collars."

She leaned toward me, and began to whisper.

Hours later, after Maira had told me everything she knew and we'd waited through countless fights, the guard stomped toward me. Maira had already fought and left, so it'd just been Cade and me, waiting.

The setting sun blazed behind his head, creating a red halo that made him glow like the devil.

"You're up," he growled.

I stood. Cade joined me.

The guard led us to the exit. The trainer gave us one look. "Try not to die."

"Aw, you like us already?" I asked.

He spat. "Nah, you're good entertainment. You piss off the Ring Master."

True enough. I saluted, then stepped out into the middle of the arena, Cade at my side.

The crowd roared, sending adrenaline buzzing through me, followed by a bit of fear. That Dark Magic-Land octopus had nearly killed us last time. Hiding my magic was all well and good until it got me in a situation like that.

I scanned the crowd, looking for Cocidius and Rowan. I swore I could feel her presence.

"Into the middle!" the trainer shouted.

We strode across the dirt toward the middle of the ring as I kept searching the stands. On the far side, one of the great stone platforms was relatively empty. There were two chairs, one far larger than the other.

Cocidius slouched in the larger one, his golden horns gleaming in the light of the setting sun. Rage swelled in my chest, hot and fierce, but the sight of Rowan distracted me.

She looked the same.

My sister.

No longer covered in the black oil of the enchantment, she was pale as ever, with her mahogany hair and blue eyes. She didn't look at me—not that she could recognize me with the glamour I'd used my illusion to create—but I ached to call out to her.

"She's here," Cade murmured.

"I need to get close. I want to see if she's enchanted." There might not even be visible signs, but I had to check.

"Maybe during the fight. I'll do what I can to make it happen."

"Thank—"

The Ring Master bellowed into the arena. "Welcome, one and all!"

The soldiers in the crowd howled. Cocidius sat silently, eyes glued to us. I shivered. If he saw through my glamour—or I dropped it—he'd know immediately who we were. He'd seen us during the fight at the Phoenician temple.

I glanced at Cade, pleased to see that he still looked different. His magic was tightly tamped down as well.

The Ring Master turned to us. "You have one job. Kill the monsters. There will be weapons."

"What the heck?" I muttered.

Then the world exploded in a green flash. Something invisible grabbed me around the waist and yanked me backward, throwing me to the ground.

The air rushed from my lungs. My chest ached as I stared up at the slowly darkening sky. Grass waved above me, along with skinny tree branches and bushes.

Aching, I pushed myself upright. I was in some kind of forest, or jungle. Weird plants I'd never seen clogged my surroundings, making it impossible to see anything more than three feet away.

"Cade?"

Silence.

I'd been dragged away from him. And the Ring Master had created a weird jungle. I looked up, catching sight of the spectators looking down on us. From their higher vantage points, they could see us. But down here, I couldn't see Cade. Or the monsters.

Understanding dawned. "Those bastards."

They wanted me to kill Cade by mistake. They'd send monsters in here—I was sure of it—but I could hardly see anything around me. I was just as likely to kill Cade as I was a beast.

Oh man. That saying "look before you leap" had never been so serious. I couldn't just throw myself into the fight now, attacking without thought. I could take out Cade.

That meant my lightning power was out of the question.

Anxiety rose in my chest, a prickly feeling that made my breath come short. I was helpless out here. I could draw my sword, but then they'd know I had that power.

They'd said there would be weapons.

Slowly, I climbed to my feet, my ears perked for any noise. The rustling of the leaves, the roar of the crowd, but nothing else.

How was I supposed to hear anything over those jerks?

I crept through the bushes, eyes alert.

I caught sight of a glint of metal lodged in a bush and hurried over, trying to keep my feet silent.

Please be a sword.

It was a bow and arrow.

"Bastards." I grabbed the arrow, ignoring the bow. Of course they gave me a long distance weapon. Perfect for mistakenly shooting Cade.

A low growl sounded. I whirled, arrow raised.

The beast leapt at me from the bushes. It was the size of a large jungle cat, but looked like a massive reptile. A dinosaur, almost.

My heart jumped into my throat as I called on my lightning power—now that I could see him, I could strike. But the beast collided with me before I could get so much as a spark.

Its claws dug into my shoulders as it threw me to the ground.

I grunted, raising my arrow spear and stabbing the creature in the neck.

It hissed and flailed, claws digging into my flesh. I pushed off the ground, trying to get on top, but the monster was too heavy.

I yanked my arrow free and aimed for the right eye, turning my head as the arrow thudded into the squishy orb.

The creature shrieked, its claws finally releasing from my shoulders as it exploded in a poof of black dust. Black magic, not a real animal. But its claws had been real enough. Pain surged through me as I heaved it off, then scrambled to my feet.

The monster's shriek had given away my location.

I sprinted away, trying to stay silent on the forest floor. As I ran, I glanced up, trying to find Cocidius's platform. I needed to get to it. Needed to see Rowan up close.

I couldn't see them anywhere.

They were behind me, damn it.

I slowed to a stop, panting, and crouched near a bush. As my breath heaved in and out, my lungs tightened. I tried to listen for oncoming monsters, but all I could hear was my breath.

My head buzzed with fear and anxiety, a potent and unfamiliar combo.

So unfamiliar. *Too* unfamiliar.

I wasn't normally this freaked out.

I sniffed lightly, catching a scent of something strange on the air. A spell for paranoia? Maybe.

I sank lower against the bushes, hiding.

So not my usual style. I knew that, yet it was hard to help. I didn't want to kill Cade in an accidental fit of magically induced fear, and I sure as heck didn't want him to do the same to me.

My gaze darted around, landing on every fluttering leaf and waving grass.

It wasn't smart to run right up to the dais where Cocidius and Rowan could get a good look at me. Even with my glamour, it was risky. What if she sensed me? What if she was enchanted like we thought she was and she turned me over to him?

I could use my illusion to become invisible and sneak up—I could even create an illusion of myself crouching here in fear—but as long as I couldn't tell where the monsters were, they could attack my illusion and blow my cover.

My mind raced, trying to come up with a solution. Desperately trying to hear around me to figure out how many monsters were left.

I wanted to call out to Cade, but didn't dare.

Tense minutes passed as I waited, trying to hear or see with anything other than my puny human eyes.

All around, the wind rustled leaves and footsteps cracked small twigs underfoot.

Wait, footsteps?

I tilted my head, focusing on my hearing.

Use it.

Oh crap!

I listened harder. The footsteps were sixty feet away. Four of them. A beast. A hundred feet away, there were different footsteps. Two of them, creeping through the brush.

Cade.

Use it.

Cade's footsteps moved toward the creature's deliberately.

Oh my fates, a new power was coming online.

Super Hearing.

And from the way I could see the different blades of grass in the distance, vision as well. Who had the power of sight and vision?

Heimdall. The guardian of Asgard, watcher of the Bifröst, the rainbow bridge.

I could totally use this. In my hour of need, the Norse gods had given me another useful power. I perked my ears again.

Cade was showing off with the monster sixty feet away, but there were two more on the other side of the arena.

Quickly, I put my original plan into action. I created an illusion of myself, still crouched in place, while turning my real body invisible.

It was weird to look at myself, silent and still in the shadow of the bush, and I turned away quickly, hurrying through the bushes toward Cocidius's platform.

It was risky, I knew it. But I had to see Rowan. I had to know if some of my sister was still in there.

As I slipped through the bushes, I kept my hearing alert, tracking the monsters that hunted us. One was closing in on my fake self—I'd have to make her run soon—while another was near Cade.

I neared the platform with Cocidius and Rowan, slowing my steps and trying to avoid any of the bushes. I couldn't make them rustle weirdly or people might notice.

I stopped about twenty feet from the dais, squinting through the dim light. It was nearly full dark now, making it hard to see, but the sight of Rowan caught my breath.

My sister.

She was really here, and she was really alive.

But her blue eyes were cloudy.

Shit. We'd expected a spell—nothing would make her stay willingly with Cocidius—but I hated having it confirmed. This meant we'd have to find a cure, and that could be impossible.

Please let there be a cure.

I eyed her for a moment more, my heart aching, feeling like it was reaching out to her and begging her to come to her senses. To shake off the effect of the evil enchantment.

Her gaze snapped to mine.

Briefly, the clouds in her eyes cleared. They were blue again. Confusion, then fear and longing.

Could she see me?

Not likely.

Then the clouds came back. Her face smoothed out, expressionless.

I wilted, grief racing through me.

Crunching branches sounded to the right.

Shit!

I'd lost track of the monsters. A quick survey revealed that the one who had been hunting my illusion had realized it wasn't real—no smell, probably—and it'd come for me.

Invisibility only worked against the humans in the stands.

I hurried away from the dais, racing back toward my illusion. No way I could have a fight as an invisible person. It'd look really freaking weird if the dino-monsters were fighting with the air. And I needed my illusion power to stay a secret if we were to rescue Rowan and free the captives.

The monster began to pick up speed, its footsteps thundering behind me.

Shit, shit, shit.

It was still thirty feet away, but it was big. Bigger than the last, from the sound of it.

I used my illusion to make my fake self run toward me. That way, when I reappeared and made her disappear, at least it wouldn't be super obvious. I had no idea if she was really running exactly toward me. I couldn't hear an illusion that had no weight, and my understanding of the terrain in the arena was a bit off, but I prayed I'd find her before the monster caught me.

My heart thundered as I ran, sprinting across the ground. The monster gained on me, its every step closing in.

I clutched the arrow in my hand, my only weapon. I could strike with my lightning, but I'd wait. No need to let them know about my hearing.

A flash to my left caught my eye.

Myself!

The illusion was running toward me—sort of. I veered off, making her come toward me as I kept an ear out for the beast. It was harder to hear over my heaving breaths and pounding heart.

A large bush provided some cover, so I darted under it, making my illusion do the same. I pulled the switch quickly, making her disappear and my real self reappear.

The beast leapt out of the bushes a moment later, coming straight for me. I wasted no time, jumping for it instead of cowering, slamming my arrow up into its stomach.

It hissed and thrashed, jerking backward.

The arrow snapped off in its stomach.

No!

My only weapon, except my lightning. I called on it, charging it up and envisioning a great bolt striking down from the sky.

Before the lightning could shoot downward, the monster leapt on me again.

6

The monster threw me to the ground. My lightning died, shocked out of me by the jarring impact.

Up close, I could see every fang in the beast's mouth. There was a double row. I thrashed beneath the creature, kneeing it in its wounded stomach.

It hissed, hot saliva dripping onto my face. I gagged as fear rose inside me, trying to call on the lightning with every bit of magic I had. Except it was hard—this was one I'd have to practice.

The lightning merely fizzled inside me.

I went for the monster's eyes, my hand forming a claw. Before my fingers landed in the socket, the beast was yanked off of me.

I gasped, suddenly able to breathe, and watched Cade stab his arrow into the monster's throat. The beast flopped and writhed, then exploded in a cloud of magical black dust.

Panting, I scrambled to my feet. "Thanks."

"Anytime." He crouched and turned, searching for more creatures.

I cocked my head, listening. There were no more footsteps. "We got them all."

He turned and looked at me. "How can you tell?"

I pointed to my ears. "New power."

"Heimdall?"

"I think so." I joined him, standing close as we looked around. "This has to be over, right? He said one challenge."

"I would think—"

The jungle fell away from us, returning the arena to its normal barren ground. I glanced toward Cocidius, whose posture was slightly more alert, then toward the Ring Master.

Full dark had fallen, but torches had been lit around us. They illuminated his face, casting it in shades of red and orange that only highlighted the rage twisting his features.

"Whoo, boy, he's pissed all right," I said.

"He wanted us to kill each other."

"I'm not going to oblige."

The Ring Master raised his arms, and magic swirled on the air.

"Hey!" I shouted. "You said that was it for us!"

He said nothing, just gave me a look that could burn a person's soul away, and jerked his arms down.

My stomach dropped as a great black swarm formed in the air, hopping over us. I squinted upward, trying to see what it was.

"Giant wasps," Cade said. "Thousands."

Panic leapt in my chest. "How do we fight a swarm?"

One monster, fine. But thousands? This was where Ana would create a shield. But we had no Ana.

Shit, shit, shit.

The wasps swarmed in the sky above, and I realized that the Ring Master was also moving his arms. Conducting them like an orchestra.

There was no water for me to call on—just the river nearby. It wasn't enough to drown them all.

I called on the lightning again, reaching for it, praying that my previous failed attempts had been practice. It sparked and burned inside me, Thor's gift reaching toward the heavens and commanding the lightning to strike.

But instead of going for the wasps—there was no way I could blast them all—I envisioned a cage of lightning surrounding us.

The light snapped down from the sky, arching over us like a dome. A cage of lightning crackled around us, nearly blinding me.

"Amazing," Cade murmured.

Strain pulled at my muscles and my will as I forced the lightning to shield us.

Something slammed against the cage wall, fizzled and burned.

The wasps.

They threw themselves at the cage. They were the size of dogs, their stingers as long as my forearm. A few shots of those and we'd be dead.

Exhaustion pulled at me as I fed my magic to the cage. My shoulder wounds ached.

I gasped. "How will we kill them all?"

Cade squinted up through the cage. "We can't kill them all, but they may have a queen. We can try for her."

"Yes!" Hope flared. "Maira said the slave collars are propelled by the magic of one source. These bastards like to use magic like that. So maybe the queen's magic controls the rest. If we can find her..."

Cade searched the sky as more and more slammed into the cage around us. Slowly, they petered off, flying higher into the sky. Waiting. Waiting.

"What are they waiting for?" I asked, anxiety ratcheting up inside me.

"Something's going to change. They don't want to decrease their numbers."

Suddenly, my lightning faltered and flickered. Then the cage disappeared, the lightning drawn back up into the sky, then outward toward the edges of the arena.

It struck against metal rods that extended high into the air.

"The bastard created lightning rods," Cade said.

And now my lightning was useless.

And the wasps were hurtling down toward us. A big one led the charge.

I pointed. "The queen!"

"Shield me with your illusion," he said. "I'm shifting forms."

I didn't have time to guess at what he planned, but I followed on instinct, using the last of my drained magic to create a mirror image of human Cade as he shifted into his wolf form. Immediately, I hid the wolf from the eyes of the crowd. Fortunately, the wasps created a shield over us so that they couldn't see well.

Unfortunately, they were super close. My skin was ice and my brain buzzed with fear. I'd never been so scared in my life.

The queen was fifteen feet above me when her giant body collapsed in on itself, blood spraying. I couldn't see Cade because of the illusion, but I knew what he'd done.

Cade had jumped up and bitten her.

Holy crap.

Quickly, I formed an illusion of lightning striking down to where the queen now thrashed in the air, no doubt being shaken in Cade's wolf jaws. It looked like the lightning struck the queen—hopefully the crowd would buy it.

Suddenly, the wasps all disappeared.

The queen was dead.

Warm, heavy fur pressed against my side. Cade. He shifted

back to human, his arm on my shoulder, and I used the last of my illusion power to make his fake form disappear.

We stood, panting.

Fading adrenaline made my limbs weak, and I leaned against Cade.

"The lightning illusion was smart," he said.

I nodded, my breaths heaving. "Thanks. I didn't know how we'd explain their death otherwise."

"And now they just think you're a powerful lightning mage—or that his rods stopped working."

"We need all our powers to stay secret. I don't want them tying us up in that magical rope again if they suspect what we are."

He nodded.

The Ring Master stepped up to the edge of his platform, scowling. He was about to speak when clapping sounded.

I turned toward it.

Cocidius.

"Just you wait, buddy," I muttered.

The Ring Master closed his mouth and stepped back.

I took that as our cue. "Let's go."

We limped off the field. Blood seeped slowly from my wounds, and I was exhausted. As I neared the exit, I glanced back at Rowan.

She and Cocidius disappeared, leaving their dais empty.

I felt her loss in my chest. Panic welled. I gripped Cade's arm. "She's gone."

"She'll be back." He lowered his voice since we were near the trainer. "We're too weak now to save her, anyway."

I leaned against him, acknowledging his words.

The trainer stepped back to let us inside the corral. It was empty now, since we were the last fighters. He jerked his head toward the exit. "To the healer."

I grimaced, but did as he said. I knew I didn't have the strength left to heal myself. And what little I did have, I needed to save for our rescue attempt.

"We'll have to take our chances."

"Yeah."

Three guards escorted us to the healer's—more than before, which meant they were growing wary of us. Good thing we hadn't used all our skills. If they'd known the magic that was going on behind the scenes during that fight, our guard would be twice as big.

My stomach turned as we entered her creepy roundhouse and took our seats. She stood with her back to us, stirring her glowing cauldron.

"Wonder how long she'll make us wait?" I muttered.

Boris the rat popped out of her hair as if he'd heard us, glittering eyes glued to us. He chittered, patting the healer on the head with one front paw.

"Calm down, Boris," she croaked.

Boris squeaked again.

"Don't you know this potion is important?" she said. "We need it for the collars. No collars, no slaves. Then we're doing our own laundry."

I doubted the captives washed her laundry much, given the look of her, but that wasn't the interesting part.

This must've been the potion that kept the collars' magic powered up. Suddenly, I was grateful that the dino-beast had dug into me.

We'd just found the location of the collars' source magic.

Boris leapt off her head and ran across the floor to us. His fur shined a dark brown, and he actually wasn't a bad-looking rat.

He stopped near us and sat up on his hind legs, whiskers twitching.

"How you doing?" I asked.

He inclined his head, inspecting our wounds. My shoulders looked a bit like ground meat, which made my stomach turn, and Cade had a deep laceration in his side.

Boris turned on his hind legs and ran to the side of the house, where a tall shelf contained various vials and glowing objects. This place would be creepy-cool in a Halloween way if the healer weren't such a miserable witch.

Boris grabbed a vial in his mouth and brought it back to us, dropping it at our feet. I leaned down to pick it up as he repeated the gesture, bringing a second vial.

I uncorked it and sniffed.

"Smells good," I murmured. "Comforting."

Cade sniffed his. "Healing potion. Thank you, Boris."

I downed the contents in one gulp, enjoying the taste of berries. "You're a good rat, Boris."

Maybe he'd liked our compliments on our last visit, I didn't know. But I'd take it.

As I set the vial on the bench next to me and stood, the healer turned.

"Back again, are you?" she said.

"And leaving just as quickly." I nodded to Boris. "Great rat you have there."

She glared at Boris. "Again?"

He shrugged, a movement that clearly said, "If you're not going to do it, I am."

We left her sputtering at the rat and him ignoring her, and stepped outside. The three guards waited, their gazes riveted to the door.

They escorted us to the food hall, which was mostly empty. No Maira. Cade and I ate quickly, restoring a good bit of our strength, then were escorted to our roundhouse. Exhaustion pulled at me as I walked, and I had to use every bit of magic I had to maintain the glamour that we wore.

There were more guards on the roundhouse this time. Four at least, depending on how many of our escorts stayed.

They shoved us inside and slammed the door behind us.

I turned to Cade. "Rowan is gone from the camp."

"She'll return. Have faith. This is his headquarters."

"Where would they go?"

"To meet with the other Rebel Gods, possibly."

I nodded, pacing.

"Rest. Gain your strength. We'll find her."

I nodded, praying they would return. Reluctantly, I lay on the furs and stared at the ceiling, trying to relax so that my magic would regenerate.

Cade lay next to me, and I reached for his hand. "Thank you for all of this. I know it's your job, but thank you."

"It is my job. But I'm here because of you." He turned his head to look at me. "I care for you, Bree. More than I've ever cared for anybody. That means I care for your sister as well. We'll save her. Promise."

Tears pricked my eyes. It'd been so long since I'd had anyone at my side besides Ana and Rowan.

Now I had the Protectorate, but even better, I had Cade.

I leaned my head toward his shoulder and rested, letting my magic fill up inside me. Every second that passed was an eternity, but he was right. I needed to recover.

I felt her return to the camp like I'd been struck by lightning. I sat upright, gasping.

"She's here?" Cade asked.

"I can feel her."

"Good." He climbed to his feet. "I'm ready to fight. Are you?"

"Definitely." My magic wasn't at 100 percent, but it was close enough. I walked to the door and pressed my ear to it, calling upon my new hearing power from Heimdall. The sound of men's breathing filtered through the door, and I counted. "Four of them."

"It'd be best if we could get them in here to take them out. There'd be some sound muffling from the walls and no witnesses."

"Agreed." I stepped back from the wall. "But how?"

He rubbed his chin, brow creased.

A half second later, Mayhem flew in through the back wall, as if she'd been listening to us.

I grinned. "Hey there."

She wagged her tail. For the first time, she had no ham or hunk of meat in her mouth. She was ready for battle. I wouldn't put it past her to have a battle ham, but today she flew solo.

"Could you lead the guards in here?" I asked her.

She nodded, then flew out the back wall again. Cade and I took up position on either side of the door so we could jump them. I drew my sword from the ether, and he did the same. I met his gaze, and he grinned.

Now it was really time to fight, something that the god of war definitely enjoyed.

I didn't bother to give us the usual glamour. This was it— now or never. Cocidius was going to figure out we were after him, so no need to waste my magic.

And I'd be glad to fight beside Cade when he actually looked like the guy I knew.

There were some confused murmurs, then Mayhem flew through the front door a moment later.

The door slammed open, and two men rushed in.

I took the first one, slicing my blade across his throat before he realized what was happening. Cade did the same with the second.

The last two guards were harder. They'd seen their fellows fall.

I lunged out of the door and grabbed one by the shirt, yanking him inside and plunging my blade into his gut. He gurgled and spat blood as I twisted the blade.

Normally I'd feel bad about killing a non-demon, but these guys participated in slavery and forced captives into death fights.

I hated taking a life, but these guys were fair game.

Cade went for the last guard, cutting off his shout of alarm before it could get too loud. He dragged the guard's limp body into the roundhouse and nodded at Mayhem. "Good job."

She nodded enthusiastically, looking like she wanted to give a yip of excitement. But she bit it back, now a seasoned war dog.

War dogs...

"Cade," I whispered. "What about the war dogs? The ones who hunted us?"

He looked at Mayhem. "Can you go distract them so they don't let up the alarm? They might not sense us, but just in case."

Mayhem nodded and zoomed out of the house, ready to take care of her fellow canines.

"Handy to have a pug dragon," I said.

"Very." Cade crept to the edge of the door and peered out. "The torches are all doused, and the camp is quiet."

"There will be sentries."

"They may be asleep. But can you conceal us?"

I reached into my pocket, making sure I still had the heavenly transport charm. "Yes. But we should hold hands since we can't see each other."

He shifted his sword to his other hand and reached for mine. I gripped his palm, then used my magic to make us invisible. It shivered over us.

"To the fighters' quarters first," I said. "We'll release them so they can break into the armory. When we've got Rowan, I'll set up the alarm, and they can start to fight."

"I'll stay with them and see it done, then join you back at the Protectorate."

"You're really sure that same portal will be there?"

He nodded. "It's been there thousands of years. I have faith."

"Good. Then let's go."

We crept out of the roundhouse, keeping our footsteps as silent as we could. The village was eerily quiet at this hour, the total lack of sounds of modern life making it feel weird.

We passed several smaller roundhouses before finding the large one at the edge of the village. It looked just as Maira had described, down to the worn-out track leading from the door. The track that hundreds of fighters had trod before being forced to fight for their lives so that Cocidius would have some entertainment.

Rage burned in my chest, a renewed commitment to take the bastard out. And everyone who participated in this miserable operation.

It was truly the worst of humanity, a stew of violence and aggression that did nothing good for the world.

"Lighten up," Cade whispered.

I realized that I was squeezing the hell out of his hand and loosened my grip.

There were only two guards at the door, which didn't seem like many until I saw the massive wooden bar.

No way the prisoners could get out to overtake the guards.

"I'll take the left," I murmured.

Cade let go of my hand, and we split up, each of us heading for our guard. I raised my sword and sliced him right through the throat. I really needed to start mixing up my kill shots, but this one was just so effective.

He fell to the ground, gurgling on his own blood.

Cade's guard fell silently as well, and we lifted up the heavy bar that kept the door locked.

When I opened the door and saw all the fighters trapped inside, caged animals just waiting for a fight to the death, I didn't feel guilty about killing the guards.

We were going to take these bastards out.

7

Maira hurried to the door, grabbing one of the fallen guards by the foot and dragging his body inside. Cade hauled the other one in after them.

I followed them into the house and dropped our invisibility illusion, revealing ourselves.

The fighters gathered around us, twenty in all. Confusion flickered on some faces, but most seemed to realize what the deal was.

"These are the ones I told you about," Maira said.

"How can we trust them?" grumbled a man. It was the same one from the first meal—the suspicious-looking one who hadn't spoken.

"I just risked my life to save you," I said.

Cade stepped forward, dropping the control he'd kept over his magic. His signature surged forward, the sound of clashing swords, the scent of a storm at sea, and the aura of black and silver.

A low gasp ran through the crowd, mirroring my own. It'd been a while since I'd felt the full extent of Cade's power, and... *dang.*

"I am Belatucadros." His voice was quiet, but powerful.

Shock painted people's faces.

"I will finish Cocidius," Cade said. "He is not what a god should be."

There was a murmur of agreement and then silence.

I looked at everyone. "We are going to rescue my sister and ambush Cocidius. It will not take long, but we need your silence until then. Go to the armory and get weapons."

Everyone nodded, clearly excited about the plan.

I looked at Maira. "I've learned where they store the potion that fuels the slave collars. The healer makes it in a cauldron. It's in her roundhouse."

"I'll take care of that," Maira said. "And I found out that Cocidius sleeps in the roundhouse at the east side of camp. There will be a couple of guards, and his sigil is carved on the door."

I nodded. "Thank you, and good luck. I will send the signal —a lightning bolt—when it is time to begin. Then, fight for your lives."

"We're very familiar with that," Maira said.

I smiled wryly, then turned and left, Cade at my side. Right before we stepped out the door, I reached for his hand and reignited our invisibility. It was becoming so much more natural, and I had to say that Loki's power was probably my favorite.

We hurried silently across the camp, avoiding the dog cages where Mayhem glowed like a ghost, distracting the other dogs with her antics. They couldn't figure out what she was, it seemed, but they certainly didn't hate her.

When I caught sight of Cocidius's roundhouse, I ducked behind a cart full of hay, tugging Cade along with me. He crouched beside me.

"Only two," I muttered. "Cocky bastard."

"He's got the strength of a god," Cade said. "No one else can defeat him."

"Except us."

"And we will."

I let go of his hand and called my twin daggers from the ether. "I'm going to take them out with my daggers. Follow me once they fall."

"I'll catch them before they hit the ground."

I nodded, appreciating his speed and forethought. Didn't want to alert Cocidius, after all.

"See ya'." I darted out from behind the cart and lined up my shot, then nailed both the guards in their necks. They gurgled, reaching for their wounds.

Wind brushed by me. Cade running.

The men sagged in midair, then slowly lowered to the ground, an invisible Cade easing them down. I hurried to join them, and pressed my ear against the door.

I heard nothing but the slow breathing of sleep. Two people.

"They must have returned and gone to sleep," I whispered against Cade's ear.

He nodded, and we slipped inside the roundhouse.

My heart thundered so loudly in my ears that I couldn't believe I didn't wake them. But Cocidius slept soundly on a massive pile of furs.

Rowan slept nearby on a smaller pile, a heavy chain extending out from beneath her blanket.

Rage surged through me.

I dropped my invisibility and pointed to the chain, making sure that Cade saw it.

He nodded and walked over on silent feet, picking it up and snapping it like it was made of thread. The slight jingle of metal links made Rowan twitch, then sit upright.

Cade lunged, sliding his hand over her mouth. Her wide eyes met mine as I hurried over, praying for her to recognize me.

She did, her blue eyes flaring with joy and hope.

I nodded at Cade, and he dropped his hand and drew his sword, going toward Cocidius's bedside. I looked back at Rowan, pulling the heavenly transport charm from my pocket.

Her gaze flashed to it, then clouded again.

No!

I lunged for her, trying to smack a hand over her mouth. She screamed before I could manage, the curse making her a slave to Cocidius's will.

The god leapt up before Cade could reach him, drawing a sword from the ether. Cade struck with his own blade. Steel clashed against steel. Magic surged in the air. Two gods, blade to blade. Magic to magic. The force of it nearly sent me to my knees.

Gasping, I threw my arms around Rowan so she couldn't escape.

She thrashed as I hurled the heavenly transport charm on the ground. Golden smoke billowed up. I dragged her into it, determined to save her whether she wanted it or not.

Cade could handle Cocidius, but only I could save my sister.

She thrashed and struggled, but I yanked her into the smoke. The tug of the ether pulled at me. A sense of victory soared in my chest.

I could save her.

But I stopped dead, unable to enter the ether.

Rowan pulled hard in the other direction, away from the portal.

That was impossible! She shouldn't be able to fight its pull. I tightened my grip on her, trying to drag her through the temporary portal with me.

But she was stuck, as if something chained her to this realm. I glanced at her feet, looking for another chain.

Her elbow slammed into my head, and stars danced in my eyes. My breath heaved as I struggled, panic beating at my chest. I pulled harder, feeling like I was being torn in two by the pull of Rowan and the portal, both of which fought against each other.

Over her shoulder, Cade and Cocidius fought viciously, both of their wounds flowing with blood. They were very evenly matched, though Cade looked like he had a slight edge.

We had this! If only I could get Rowan away from here.

But some dark magic kept her from entering the portal. She was trapped here, somehow. Terrible dread weighed down my stomach.

Five guards rushed in, so fast that they had to have some kind of super speed. In a flash, they overpowered Cade. Just briefly. Just long enough for Cocidius to lunge for us.

He grabbed Rowan around the waist, yanking her away with his superior strength. Several strands of her hair came away in my hand, and she yelped in pain.

Cade broke away from the new attackers as Cocidius hurled a transport charm to the ground. Golden dust billowed into the room. He dragged Rowan through.

Away.

"No!" I raced after them, about to hurl myself into the portal.

Cade grabbed me around the waist. "Stop! You could end up in another god's realm with no way to escape."

"But Rowan!"

"You can't rescue her if you're a captive yourself. Or dead."

He was right. Entering an unknown godly realm was a suicide mission.

And we had to save the captives here. I had made a promise. If I leapt into that portal, Cade would follow me. The people here needed us.

I shoved the strands of Rowan's hair into my pocket—it was creepy, but it was the only physical part of Rowan I could hang onto—and drew my sword from the ether.

The guards who had attacked Cade rounded the edge of the now fading portal, their gazes on us.

"You bastards." Rage flowed through me. Their interruption had given Cocidius the upper hand. He'd stolen my sister *again.*

I didn't even bother to strike with my sword. I called the lightning from the sky. It cracked so loudly my head rang, spearing through the thatched roof and filling the room with a blinding white burst.

It struck them all dead in one blow.

Overhead, the thatch roof flamed. The red glow flickered on the crispy bodies of my enemies, and I left them to fry.

"I'm going to burn this whole place down." Anger seethed in my voice, and I strode from the flaming roundhouse.

I called on my wings, exhilaration shooting through me as they unfurled from my back.

I launched myself into the sky, observing the chaos down below. My lightning strike had been the signal, and the fight had begun.

On the west side of the village, the fighters were trying to break into the armory. Those who had magic—fire and ice— were using it to take out the guards who blocked the way.

"Cade!" I shouted. "Go west, to the armory!"

He sprinted in that direction, moving so quickly he was almost a blur. They'd have their weapons soon enough.

I scanned the rest of the village, catching sight of Maira's blond head. She grappled with three guards, managing to light one on fire with her magic. I swooped toward her, directing my lightning at the other two.

They lit up like electric popsicles, and a joyful vengeance

surged through me. It was an uncomfortable sensation. It was so wrong. I didn't want to enjoy it. But I did.

I landed in front of Maira, who watched me with wide eyes. "You really are as powerful as you said."

I nodded. All around, people wearing collars peered out of buildings. "Let's go destroy this damned potion."

She grinned.

We turned and hurried the last few feet to the healer's hut. The door swung open, revealing an empty space within.

"The bitch fled into the woods," Maira hissed.

Honestly, I was pretty happy I didn't have to face her. I had eyes only for the cauldron that glowed at the side the house.

Boris the rat stood on the bench next to it, his little paws pressed against it.

"He's trying to tip it over," Maira said.

"Then let's help him." I hurried to Boris and looked down at the tiny rat. "I always knew you were good people."

He chittered at me, clearly irritated. "Get it done, already," he was obviously saying.

I braced my hands against the rim of the cauldron that held the blue potion, my nose twitching at the disgusting scent of rotted garbage and gasoline. Maira joined me, and we heaved, straining to push over the cauldron.

It tilted, little by little, until it finally crashed to its side, spewing the contents over the floor. I ran around to the front of it, peering inside. A silver collar lay at the bottom.

"Light it up," I said.

Maira shot her fire at the potion, which ignited immediately.

I looked at Boris. "Can you show me which ones are the healing potions?"

As the fire burned, devouring the potion, Boris ran to the shelves. He hopped onto them, chittering and pointing. I filled up a bag with them. My years scavenging to survive, particularly when we were young, made me loath to leave anything of value behind.

"What are you doing?" Maira asked.

"We need to be able to heal the wounded. Come on, fill a bag."

We worked quickly, taking everything of value that Boris pointed out. When we were done, I turned back to the cauldron. The room was smoky and hot as hell, but the potion was nothing but blackened char. Inside the tipped over cauldron, the silver collar was a lump of melted metal.

"Perfect." I grinned, satisfaction coursing through me.

We ran from the house, Boris jumping onto my shoulder as I passed through the door.

Outside, the people wearing collars were pulling them off. They'd unsnapped once the magic had broken.

"Finally," Maira said. She hurried toward one of the people and handed off the two bags of potions that we'd collected. "These are for the wounded. Protect them. Give them out when you can."

The woman nodded vehemently. "I will."

Maira turned back to me. "I'll see you when this is over."

"When we're victorious." I shot into the air, Boris hanging onto my shoulder and chittering away in my ear. "Probably should have caught a ride with someone else, pal."

His annoyed squeaks said he agreed, but he clung fast to my shoulder.

I hovered in the air, taking in the scene. Cade stormed through the village, his sword drawn. He took out a soldier every three seconds on average, moving faster than anyone I'd ever seen. Mayhem had left the dogs and now blew fire at any soldier she could find, chasing them through the village.

Near the armory, the fighters used their stolen weapons. They swung swords, fired arrows, defended with shields, and stabbed with pikes. On the other side of the village, soldiers were harassing the slaves who'd worn the collars, trying to round them up.

Ruthlessly, I struck them down with lightning.

"Your reign of terror is *over*," I screamed, so loudly that I shocked even myself.

Most looked up toward me, and I wondered what I looked like, flying in the sky on enormous wings of silver as lightning struck all around me.

"Run or *die*!" I yelled.

Most didn't run, so I struck them down with lightning, guilt and satisfaction streaking through me. It was a gross combo. In a sense, it was good. For every evil soldier that fell, a former captive *wasn't* being killed.

Still, I hated it.

I steeled myself, though, determined to finish the job.

Finally, the last of the soldiers had fled. The rest were dead. The woman with the bag of potions raced through the village, handing them out to the wounded. I tried to count the wounded as I landed near Cade and Maira, but it was too dark to see without my lightning.

Boris immediately leapt from my shoulder onto Cade, clearly preferring someone without wings. Fair enough. Rats weren't meant to fly.

Blood streaked Maira's face and poured from a wound on her arm. But her eyes were bright with joy.

"We did it," she said. "*You* did it."

"We all did." I looked around as people gathered near. When it seemed like everyone was there, I spoke. "We didn't kill Cocidius. I am sorry. But we will. Soon. He will never return here, and I will destroy this war camp so it cannot be re-used."

"You can return home," Cade said.

Smiles broke out amongst the crowd, then cheers and shouts.

"Leave here soon," I said. "Gather your things so that I can destroy the buildings."

Everyone nodded, shouting thanks before departing. Maira lingered.

"Do you want to come with us?" I asked. "There's a portal to Earth."

She shook her head. "I have family in my village. And I want to see to it that everyone returns safely. Some have been prisoners for years. They'll need help finding their way home."

I nodded, hugging her.

"Thank you," she said.

"Thank you." I pulled back. "We couldn't have done it without you."

"Come back and visit, if you like."

"I just might."

She looked at Cade. "You're a proper god."

He grinned and inclined his head.

She smiled at us, then turned and left. I stood next to Cade and Boris. Mayhem joined us. Once everyone had cleared out of the buildings, I struck each one with lightning, setting it aflame.

Last, I used my lightning to explode each of the rock platforms that made up the arena. Soon, it was nothing but rubble.

As I looked at the destruction surrounding us, satisfaction surged through me. I looked at Cade. "Let's get out of here."

We arrived back at the Protectorate exhausted and filthy. It'd taken us hours to find the portal again, but at least Cade had one transportation charm left once we arrived at Hadrian's Wall. It allowed us to cover the last several hundred miles home quickly.

We appeared on the front lawn as dawn was peeking over the horizon. The castle's windows glowed with warm golden light as gloaming turned to morning.

"Never seen anything look so good," Cade said.

"I could eat a literal ton of food."

We started for the stairs, Mayhem zipping off to immediately alert our friends that we were home. Boris chittered happily as we walked into the foyer.

"I don't think he liked being the healer's assistant," Cade said.

"It looks like we have a new friend."

Ana raced down the sweeping staircase, her gaze riveted to me. Cass followed her. They were both dressed in the same clothes as before, a clear indicator that they'd been busy this whole time as well. "Did you find her?"

"Yes. But I couldn't save her. Not yet." The disappointment that welled in me was reflected in Ana's eyes.

She shook it away. "That's okay. We will."

"Did you have any luck?"

She nodded. "Yes. Cass helped me find the entrance to the goddess's realm. We think she is Eris, the Greek goddess of discord and strife. But let's call a meeting. The others will want to hear."

I nodded, and thanked Cass, who smiled.

"Where's Caro?" I asked. "Didn't she go with you?"

"Yeah, but we ran into a sticky situation, and she got hit with a fireball," Ana said. "She's fine, just getting patched up."

The things our friends risked for us…

Damn, we were lucky.

Mayhem zipped back through the room. "Did you find Jude and Hedy?"

She yipped.

"Can you tell them to meet us in the kitchen?" I thought my

stomach was going to devour itself. Using all that magic—and the stress of losing Rowan—had left me famished.

Mayhem yipped again, and flew off.

We hurried down the stairs into the kitchen, where Hans bustled around the stove, his white apron covered in dusty flour.

A fire burned in the large hearth, and copper pans hung from the ceiling. The scent of freshly baked bread made my mouth water.

Hans looked up and grinned. "You look awful. Sit at the table."

"Thanks, Hans."

I lowered my aching body into a seat at the heavy round table in front of the hearth. Ana, Cass, and Cade joined me. Boris leapt onto the table, nose twitching.

"New friend?" Ana asked.

"Yep." I rubbed his head with a single finger.

"I've got a couple of rat buddies you might like, Boris," Cass said. "Ralph and Rufus."

Boris tilted his head, considering.

Hans appeared with great bowls of steaming stew which caught Boris's attention. New friends were interesting, but food was better.

Hans set the stew in front of us, along with bread and butter. Finally, glasses of red juice. He shook his finger at all of us. "Don't forget your juice. Vitamins."

I grinned. Boris chittered.

"I wouldn't forget you," Hans said. "I do not know who you are, but you are clearly a friend."

He laid a little platter of cheese in front of Boris, who squeaked with delight.

We dug in, silently chowing down as memories of the fight rushed through my head. Ana was eating just as fast as we were.

"Did you just return?" I asked.

She nodded and swallowed. "We found a lead."

"Good."

Jude and Hedy hurried into the room, their eyes bright. Ali and Haris followed behind, dark circles under their eyes.

"Well?" Jude said.

"How did it go?"

I reached into my pocket and pulled out the few strands of mahogany hair, laying them on the table. "That's all I have of my sister."

"But she's alive?" Hedy asked.

"Yes." I explained to them what had happened.

"It sounds like there was a joining spell on her," Hedy said. "She's connected to Cocidius—maybe even the other gods—and cannot leave his side without his permission. You won't be able to rescue her until you break the spell."

"Which means that when she was attacking us in the fae realm, she had his permission to be there," Ana said.

"Exactly," Jude said.

"Is that why her eyes grow cloudy sometimes and she doesn't recognize me?" I asked.

"So she does recognize you other times?" Hedy asked.

"Yes. Briefly, in flashes."

Hedy smiled. "That's good. No, it's *excellent*. It means she's fighting the spell. She's trying to get away from him, to disobey his influence. Her strength increases your chances of success."

Both Ana and I sagged in relief. If Rowan's strength could help us, that was great. She had always been the strongest.

"How do we break the spell?" Cade asked.

Hedy pointed to the hairs. "Those will help. We may be able to get an idea of what the spell was if there's still a trace of the magic on them. Just a hint is all we need."

"Can you do that?" I asked.

"I have someone," Hedy said. "Melusine, in The Vaults."

I'd met the Ecklektica before. Just once, while visiting her shop.

Boris finished his cheese and hopped over to Hedy. She petted his head, and his little eyes closed.

Jude looked at Ana and Cass. "So you found the bloody goddesses realm?"

"Yep," Ana said. "It's on the island of Despotiko, in Greece. The entrance is through a temple that was built to worship Eris, the Greek goddess of strife. Apparently she would visit battlefields just because she liked it. Maybe that's why she's covered in blood."

"We didn't enter her realm, though," Cass said. "That would be asking for trouble. But the place is totally abandoned now. Just a rock in the middle of the sea. No one living there."

"And we don't want them knowing we're coming," Ana said.

"Exactly." Jude nodded, then turned to Haris and Ali. "And you two?"

"We've narrowed the snowy god down to Chernobog, a West Slavic deity from the twelfth century AD," Haris said. "But as for the entrance to his realm, we have only determined that it is somewhere in Germany. The north, most likely."

"I can help you," Cass said. "Sounds like you have enough clues for me to get started."

Haris grinned, dark eyes shining. "Aye, if you'd pull a bloodhound on this, we'd appreciate it."

Pull a bloodhound? I chuckled softly.

Cass inclined her head. "Anytime."

Excellent. That meant we had a lead on Eris, and we were about to have one on Chernobog. If I could just figure out which spell she was under, I could have my sister back.

It was almost too good to believe.

8

After a night of fitful sleep—which was necessary because my magic was totally drained from the fight in Cocidius's realm—Cade, Ana, and I went to The Vaults. We made our way quickly through the underground streets towards Melusine's shop.

Ana looked around with wide eyes, taking in the buildings built right into the rocks. "This place is creepy. But awesome."

"Agreed." I sidestepped a wizard who stank of black magic.

We continued up the street, until Cade stopped in from of the door to MADAME MYSTICAL'S MAGICAL MEMENTOS and held it open for us.

I glanced at Ana. "Don't call her Madame Mystical. You'll regret it."

"Personal experience?"

"Fortunately not, but after meeting Melusine, I believe the girl who gave me the advice."

I stepped inside the shop, immediately enjoying the interior. We'd never been big shoppers—never had the money—but this place was downright cool. The main room was three stories high, with illusions of pixies fluttering near the domed ceiling.

Bookshelves full of fabulous objects edged the walls all the way to the top, and the middle was a sunken area filled with low display cases and chairs.

Movement toward the back caught my eye. High up, Melusine clung to a ladder that reached three stories up. Her flame red hair tumbled down her back, glinting against the deep green catsuit that she wore. It shimmered like emeralds, complementing her gleaming stilettos.

"Wow," Ana murmured. "She's got style."

"Yep." It wasn't our style, but I liked it all the same. The red and green made her look a bit like a Christmas tree, but she really rocked it.

Quickly, Melusine slid down the ladder, pulling a complicated maneuver that I'd never manage in heels.

She turned to us and grinned, her black eyes sparkling. "What brings you back again so soon?"

"We're here about a spell." I stepped forward, crossing the space between us.

Cade must have entered behind us, because her gaze snapped from me to him, and her grin widened even more.

Suddenly, I didn't exist in Melusine's world. Neither did Ana.

"She could do a toothpaste commercial," Ana said, not bothering to lower her voice. It wasn't like Melusine would notice us.

As expected, Melusine didn't so much as glance at us again. "Well, well. Cade. So nice to see you."

"Hello, Melusine." His voice was brisk but polite. "We're hoping that you can help us."

"Anything for you," she purred.

I sighed, and walked up to stop right in front of her. Reluctantly, her gaze left Cade—he hung behind a bit; smart man—and met mine.

"What kind of spell?" Her voice had lost some of its warmth

—which was fine, because it'd basically been on fire—but she was still friendly enough.

I pulled an envelope from my pocket and handed it over. "There are a few hairs in there. The owner is enchanted with a joining spell of some kind. We'd like to know what it is exactly so that we can break it."

She frowned, brow creasing. "That's serious. Let's go."

She turned sharply on her heel and went to the back room where she conducted her magic. The small space was similar to the one we'd just left, but relatively empty. A round table in the middle held a stone basin.

I followed Melusine to the table, Ana at my side. Cade stopped by the door, no doubt conscious of not distracting Melusine, who peeked inside the envelope, then drew out a single hair.

"I'm going to see what I can find from this one," she said. "It could destroy it, but it looks like there are about five more in there."

"That's fine."

She nodded, handed the envelope back to me, then dropped the single hair into the water basin. Melusine was part Selkie, and as such, drew some of her magic from the water.

I held my breath as I watched her hover her hand over the gleaming surface. Next to me, Ana did the same, leaning forward to get a better look.

The water glowed white briefly, then a sickly yellow, then a deep red. Like blood.

Melusine sighed and stepped back, her brow wrinkled. "This is outside of my area. But I think I know someone who can help."

"Who?"

"Wait here, and you'll see." She spun and walked to the wall, pressing her hand against it.

"She likes things to be cryptic, huh?" Ana whispered.

"Seems so."

Beneath Melusine's palm, the wall glowed with a pale light, then disappeared entirely, revealing a small alcove with a full-size mirror.

My brows rose.

Melusine tapped on the glass. "Mordaca! Aerdeca!"

I glanced at Ana. Recognition shined in her eyes, just like I was sure it shined in mine.

Mordaca and Aerdeca were Blood Sorceresses from Magic's Bend. They plied their trade in Darklane, which was essentially the Vault's counterpart across the ocean. We'd met them five years ago while helping Nix with a problem.

"They have to be the same ones, right?" Ana said.

"Have to be."

"Mordaca! Aerdeca! I know it's late, but wake up!" Melusine shouted.

Oh, right. It'd be the middle of the night over in Oregon, where Magic's Bend was located.

"I'm coming, I'm coming." An annoyed, groggy voice sounded from inside the mirror. It was a raspy voice, like that of a woman who enjoyed cigarettes and whiskey on a regular basis. For one hundred years.

A moment later, Mordaca appeared in the mirror. Her black bouffant hairdo made her look like Elvira, and somehow, she'd managed to pile on even more black eye makeup than the Mistress of the Dark. It was like a black mask that swept across her eyes. The black satin robe that she wore gleamed in the low light, and plunged deeply to reveal some seriously fabulous cleavage.

That kind of chest would get in the way of my demon killing, but she looked like a sexy, scary supermodel.

"What is it?" Mordaca asked.

"We've got a doozy of a spell over here. Something I think you can handle."

"At this hour? I was just about to go to bed."

"It seems important." Melusine shot a glance over her shoulder at me. "In fact, everything about this chick seems important."

"Who is it?" Mordaca peered around.

Could she see me out of the mirror?

Her gaze widened. "You! You're the two who helped Nix a few years ago. With your funny car."

I frowned. I'd hardly call the buggy a "funny car." But I needed her help, so I smiled and waved. "Yep. And we could really use some help if you have a chance."

She thrummed her black-painted nails against her arm. "You volunteered to help her fight Drakon, didn't you? They didn't pay you or anything, as I recall."

I shrugged. "Not for that job. Seemed like a good idea at the time."

Mordaca nodded decisively. "Fine. But Aerdeca is going to hate this. She's been asleep for hours." She leaned away from the mirror and shouted behind her. "Aerdeca! Wake up! And bring the kit!"

She turned back, grinning as she stepped out of the mirror and into Melusine's workshop. "I always kind of like doing that."

I blinked, stunned. "Whoa. What kind of mirror is that?"

"A very, very rare one," Melusine said.

"Does it go anywhere else?" I asked.

"Just to Mordaca and Aerdeca's shops. We consult on various jobs."

"Good for business." Mordaca stalked toward me, and I realized that she was wearing furry black mules with her robe. She spared one interested glance at Cade, then stopped in front of me. "What is it that you need?"

I handed her the envelope and explained the situation.

Melusine joined us. "I think it's blood magic."

Mordaca nodded. "We can figure out what it is, but it won't come cheap."

"That's fine." I didn't know where we'd get the money, but we'd manage. We'd been paid a bit by the Protectorate and still had some in our nest egg, but I'd heard about Mordaca and Aerdeca's insane prices. "Do you take credit cards?"

Cade stepped up beside me. "Cash will do?"

Mordaca grinned at him, suddenly much more interested. "Of course. Six grand, even."

"I'll go pick that up and be back in twenty minutes." He turned to go.

I grabbed his arm, my gaze meeting his. "Thank you. I'll pay you back."

He nodded and smiled, but didn't seem particularly concerned.

As he loped out of the room, another woman stepped through the mirror.

Aerdeca looked roughly as I remembered her—slim and blond, an icy version of her darker sister. Her pajamas were a classic white satin suit style, with her nails painted white to match. A black and white striped old-style doctor's bag was clutched in her hand.

"What is so important that I'm awake?" Her voice was sweet, but I knew enough not to be fooled.

Only a fool would think she was the sweet one because of her voice and penchant for white.

"A joining spell using blood magic," Mordaca said. "And I have a feeling I know which spell."

Aerdeca's brows rose. "Well that will cost a pretty penny."

"Indeed." Mordaca smiled, her blood-red lips gleaming in the light.

"I know just what I'll buy." Aerdeca strode over.

"Another white suit that looks like all the rest?" Mordaca said.

"Just because you can't tell the difference doesn't mean it's not there." She smiled sweetly at her sister. "Elvira."

I stifled a laugh.

The two of them made a great team, but sniping wasn't off the table.

Aerdeca set her doctor's bag on the edge of the round table and pulled out three daggers and an onyx bowl. Her gaze met mine. "We'll need some of your blood for this."

Normally, I'd stay the hell away from blood magic. It straddled the line between the dark and the light—the main reason that the sisters ran their shop out of Darklane—and it just seemed creepy in general.

But for Rowan?

I stuck my arm out so fast I almost punched Aerdeca in the stomach.

She raised a brow. "Enthusiastic, I see."

"I need to save my sister."

Her gaze softened, and she nodded. "This will pinch just a little."

Pain flared as she sliced the silver blade over my wrist, then tilted my arm so that blood flowed into the little basin. Once she'd collected a few drops, she handed me a white cloth and gestured to Ana. "You next."

I stepped back, keeping pressure on the wound, and watched as Aerdeca switched knives and repeated the procedure with Ana. Once she was done, she turned a fresh knife on herself, slicing into her own vein.

"Do you normally do that?" From what I'd heard, a blood sorceress didn't often use her own blood.

"Rarely." She held her dripping wrist over the bowl, then passed it over to Mordaca, who made her own contribution.

After Mordaca finished, she dug out two vials of potion—one silver and one blue. She tilted the contents into the bowl while murmuring some words I didn't recognize. Aerdeca joined her, their voices growing in volume.

Power filled the room, magic sparking across my skin. It tasted of whiskey and sounded like chirping birds. Light glowed from the bowl as Aerdeca added a single one of Rowan's hairs.

The liquid hissed and fizzled as it received the hair, sputtering in the light. Red smoke rose up, twisting in the air to form an image of a flower with five pointed petals. Liquid seemed to drip from the tips of the petals. Purple smoke formed at the center of the bloom.

Mordaca sighed. "As I thought. The Baeseldox weed."

Aerdeca set the bowl on the table, and the smoky flower disappeared.

"You make it sound like it's a bad thing," Ana said.

Aerdeca frowned. "It may not be. If you can find the weed. It's the key ingredient in a potion called *Capti Maximus.* That's the spell that has enchanted your sister. The antidote is made from the same weed. But there are very few on the planet."

"There's even a chance they aren't blooming right now," Mordaca said.

Shit. Fear made my stomach turn. "Where do we find the weed?"

"I've heard rumors that there is one in Belgium. But just rumors."

"Can you make the potion if we find the bloom?" Ana's voice was strained with worry.

"If you find the bloom, you can make the potion," Mordaca said. "Just boil one flower with a cup of water until it is deep red. Then drink."

"But it's *finding* the bloom that is hard," Aerdeca said.

"We'll find it." We had to. "Do you have any leads at all? Belgium is pretty big if you're just looking for a flower."

Aerdeca and Mordaca shared a glance.

"You can go to The Alchemist, a hotel bar in Ghent," Aerdeca said. "Ask for the Conductor. If the flower actually is in Belgium, he'll know where. You said this was for your missing sister?"

"Yes. She's been kidnapped. Missing for five years and we've finally found her."

Aerdeca nodded. "If the Conductor gives you trouble, remind him that he owes us. We're calling in our favor for the growth potion."

"For us? Thank you." My chest warmed. Then my mind caught on to what she'd said. "Growth potion?"

"He'll know what it means," Mordaca said. "But dress appropriately. The Alchemist is where the criminal underground mingles. But they do it in style. You'll need to get past the guards, so look like you belong. And don't draw attention if you don't want a fight."

"Dress appropriately like a criminal?" Ana asked.

"Criminals who wear haute couture, yes." Aerdeca smiled.

So, a dress. A fancy dress, if I had to guess. Wasn't that what haute couture meant?

I'd have to borrow one.

Cade arrived at that moment, hesitating in the doorway, likely to make sure he didn't interrupt any magic. He had an envelope in his hand, no doubt full of cash.

Mordaca's gaze landed on him, then she gestured between him and me. "You two should go. No large groups. You'd draw too much suspicion"

She was right on that.

Ana scowled. I felt for her. It couldn't be easy with her magic not yet fully manifested. With Rowan's life on the line, the stakes were the highest they'd ever been for us.

"Where are we going?" Cade asked.

"Ghent."

That night, the transport mage Emily gave Cade and me a ride to Ghent so we could conserve our transport charms, which were running precariously low.

I stared up at the fancy hotel made of red brick. "It looks like a giant gothic wedding cake."

Cade's gaze moved from the hotel to my dress, a tight black number that I'd borrowed from Caro. "You look beautiful."

I glanced down at the dress and the uncomfortable stilettos and laughed. "Better than my usual boots and leather, I guess."

"No." His gaze met mine. "That's better. But this is nice, too. Though maybe I like it because I can see more of you."

"So can the world." I tugged the top up over my boobs, which seemed determined to make an escape by any means necessary. I gave him an up and down, enjoying the sight of him in a tux.

I whistled low. Damn, if he didn't look good.

He grinned, a devilish smile that indicated he knew just what I was thinking. If this were a date, I'd drag him into a dark corner and kiss the sense out of him.

I shook my head. We were *not* here for that.

"Let's do this." I picked up my small duffel bag full of real clothes—no way I'd stay in this getup longer than I had to—and teetered across the cobblestone street toward the building. "This just reconfirms my admiration for women who can do stuff in heels. That shit is a *skill.*"

"I'm grateful I'll never have to know."

"Benefit of the patriarchy, my friend."

He grinned and nodded, stashing his duffel back behind a large potted bush. Fortunately, the street was clear so no one could see us. I added mine to his, then straightened and tugged my dress down over my butt.

Cade held out his arm, and I took it, butterflies in my stomach. I might not be comfortable in this dress, but play-acting a date was actually really nice.

We'd have to do this for real one day.

We walked toward the entrance of the hotel—the back entrance, as far as I could tell—and entered the bottom of a fabulous spiral stairwell. The thing was massive, sweeping up several stories. I clung to Cade's arm as we climbed.

"I vow to practice high heels," I muttered. "If undercover is part of the job, I need to learn to walk in these things. And maybe kill a demon with the heel."

"Both valuable skills."

"Right through the eye. It'd be gruesome, but effective."

He chuckled. "Agreed."

We reached the top, and the sound of laughing guests and clinking glassware led us toward the bar on the other side of the lobby.

"This place is fancy," I muttered. "Though, in fairness, I haven't seen much besides the Death's Door Saloon and the Whisky and Warlock. It doesn't take much to impress me."

Cade squeezed my arm against his side and led me toward the bar.

Two hulking guards stood by the entrance, their tuxes straining at the seams. They eyed us as we approached, and my heart thudded slightly harder. We didn't need any trouble here. Not at this phase of the operation. You couldn't fight your way to information—not easily at least.

I tried on my snootiest expression—I had no idea if it actually worked—and sailed through the entryway, intensely aware of their gazes burning into me.

It was an elegant space with small tables scattered around the bar. Two bartenders in sharp white shirts and black ties shook their cocktail shakers in a complicated rhythm that looked like a dance.

"I bet they could make something fabulously pink," I said. Caro had told me these guys were some of the best bartenders in the world. "Not that I should drink it right now, but..."

"We'll come back. When this is all over, we can do a vacation here."

I smiled briefly, liking the idea. "At a criminal underworld hotspot?"

I glanced around, taking in the sharp eyes of most of the guests. Supernaturals of all varieties, these people were here doing business—the kind that could get a person killed.

"Live dangerously, aye?"

"I don't need much help with that." I let go of his arm and sauntered to the bar—or at least, tried to—then leaned on it and smiled at the bartender.

It took him ages to notice me, but when he finally did, he smiled and spoke like I was the only person in the world. "And what can I do for you, miss?"

"We're here to see the Conductor."

The bartender's brows rose briefly. "Who sent you?"

"Mordaca and Aerdeca, from Darklane."

"You'll find the Conductor in the private bar. Tell one of the guards you need to see him. He'll take you there."

"Thank you."

Cade and I departed quickly. As soon as we made it out of the bar filled with mob bosses and underworld types, my shoulders relaxed slightly.

It was probably too soon to relax, though. We were going to

the private bar. Wasn't that normally where all the bad stuff happened? In a room in the back?

Cade stopped near the guard on the left. Though they were equal in height, the guard was a good hundred pounds heavier. Even his neck had bulging muscles. All the same, I'd bet money Cade could wipe the floor with him.

"We're here to see the Conductor. The bartender told us that you could be our escort," Cade said.

The guard glanced back into the bar, then nodded, seeming satisfied. "This way."

We followed him across the lobby and up another set of stone spiral stairs to a quiet room at the top. It was round, with windows on all sides. No doubt one of the gothic towers.

A man sat in a comfortable chair by the window, sipping from a glass of golden liquid. His magic radiated from him, a strong fizzing sensation that wasn't quite comfortable.

What the heck was he?

"Some people to see you, boss," our guard said.

The man looked up, keen eyes taking us in. He had to be in his fifties, with sharp features that reminded me of a ferret's.

The guard stepped out and shut the door behind him.

"Mordaca and Aerdeca sent us." I stepped forward. "We are looking for a Baeseldox weed, and they said you might have a lead on it."

"Ah. Mordaca and Aerdeca." He stroked his chin, a nerdy, villainous move I'd only ever seen in movies. Was this guy for real? He gestured toward chairs next to him. "Come closer."

I stepped forward, shivering at the weird feel of his magic. It grew stronger the nearer we got—and way less comfortable. Leave it to Aerdeca and Mordaca to hang out with weirdos like this guy.

Cade took the seat next to him, leaving me farther away. I appreciated it. "Do you know of any Baeseldox weed nearby?"

"I do. But the information will cost you."

"Mordaca and Aerdeca are calling in their favor for the growth potion. Whatever that means."

The slightest hint of a flush rose from his collar, and I suddenly got the idea. I clenched my jaw to keep from making a sound.

He nodded sharply. "There's been rumor that some Baeseldox weed is growing beneath the city castle."

"Gravensteen?" Cade asked.

"The very one. There's supposed to be an underground river and waterfall. At the base grows the flower."

"Why is it so hard to get to, then?"

"The Viscount who lives in the castle isn't keen on sharing." A wheezy chuckle escaped him. "No one has seen him in decades, and it's impossible to get into the castle. And since there are rumors of an active torture dungeon, no one is trying."

Well, *I* was going to try. With Rowan's life at stake, a measly torture dungeon couldn't keep me away.

"Do you have any ideas how we could get in?" Cade asked.

"None whatsoever. You'll have to go see what you can find." He stood, gesturing for the door. "I've fulfilled my debt to Aerdeca and Mordaca. You may go now." The words were hard.

Right. That was clear. And we'd gotten what we could from him. I stood. "Thanks."

His lips pressed together as he stared at me. No doubt this meeting hadn't gone as planned. Not that he'd had time to expect much, but he hadn't expected us to mention the growth potion, it was clear.

I made quick work getting to the door, wobbling only once. The air vibrated with magic from the bar, bringing with it a tense discomfort. Cade followed me down the stairs. We didn't hesitate as we made our way quickly across the lobby and down the main stairwell.

The night air was warm as we spilled out onto the dimly lit street. I sucked in a grateful breath. "Give me a pub any day. I don't care how good the drinks are in there."

Cade nodded. "Aye. Perhaps we'll vacation somewhere else."

My mouth quirked at the second mention of a vacation. Maybe it would really happen. Was I ready for that?

I had no idea. And right now, it didn't matter.

Outside, I sucked in a deep breath. Even the air felt cleaner out here. I hurried toward the potted bush and grabbed our bags, tossing one to Cade. "Let's find a public restroom, then go scout out the castle."

I could make us invisible—and it'd be kind of thrilling to change out in the street, even though no one could see us—but I really should save my power.

"Aye, good plan."

We hurried down the street until we found a public restroom. As fun as it'd been to wear the dress, I was glad to get back into my jeans and boots and leather jacket.

I met Cade out on the street. He was back in his black tactical gear, which was also much more suited to sneaking into a famous castle with a torture chamber.

"According to my phone, the castle is back this way," Cade said. "Let's stash our bags and go."

We hid them behind some three-dimensional wall art, then hoofed it down the street. Couples strolled along, many of them students, and musicians played beneath a bridge, making the night seem so lovely and normal.

But until I had Rowan back, *lovely* wasn't a state of affairs that I was familiar with.

"We shouldn't be far," Cade said.

About ten minutes later, an enormous castle appeared across the street. It was a hulking beast of a thing.

I shivered. "It just screams torture chamber."

"Now, now. That's just in the basement."

I chuckled as I studied the imposing front. "There are no guards."

"They don't need any. That door looks impenetrable."

"And no one in the city would mount a siege anyway. Who wants to get into the torture chamber besides us?"

"Not a clue. Let's check the walls."

We skirted around the castle, trying to look casual and keeping our distance, until we reached the back, where the river was located. Rivers flowed all through Ghent apparently, and the castle's back wall plunged right down into the murky water.

"That has some possibilities, right?" I asked.

"Let's find out."

We found a bridge to cross the water so we could check out the entire back wall. Old buildings sat on our side street, with the even more ancient castle looming in the moonlight.

"It really is a beast of a thing," I said.

"I don't think I've ever said this before, but that building is creepy."

"Ha, if it scares *you*, then I want no part of it."

But for Rowan, I'd find a way into that creepy castle, no matter what it took.

Movement at the castle wall—low down near the water—caught my eye. I dropped down behind a large bush, reaching up to drag Cade with me. He dropped silently, and we peered between the leaves.

"It's a boat," I whispered. "Coming right out of the wall."

9

"There has to be an entrance at the base of the castle wall," Cade murmured.

I squinted through the dark. That stretch of wall was in the shadow of the moonlight, which made it hard to see, but I called on the magic of Heimdall, asking my eyes to sharpen.

As my vision adjusted, shadows smoothed out and light glowed very faintly. "Yep. An arched gate."

The boat cleared the heavy metal gate and drifted into the river. The gate began to slide silently down behind it, and kept going, long after it reached the surface of the water.

"The gate goes under the water, doesn't it?" Cade asked.

"Yep. No swimming under."

"It'll be enchanted, too, I'd wager. Not that we can afford a loud break-in in the middle of the city."

"No. I don't want to fight whoever is in that castle." I squinted at the boat as it passed. It was long and low, with an open cargo section behind the driver, who sat up in the bow. The thing didn't move fast—it was impossible to in this river. Big barrels were stacked behind him. I strained my eyes in the low light, finally catching the world *Bier*. "That's a freaking beer delivery."

"Well, it is Belgium."

"Let's follow it. That boat is our ticket into the castle."

Cade grinned. "I like how you think."

We waited a while, long enough to let the boat get nearly out of sight, then hurried after it.

"Thank fates these things are slow," I muttered.

Thirty minutes later, we arrived at a large stone building with many windows. It pressed right up against the river, and the boat floated in through another gate.

There must be a lot of interior wharfs in the city.

I scanned the exterior wall that was perpendicular to the water, finally spotting a side entrance on the sidewalk. "Let's try that. This place can't be that well-guarded."

"Belgians are serious about their beer." There was humor in Cade's voice.

We hurried to the door, which was a modern metal thing set into the old stone walls. I tested it, knowing it was pointless. Yep. It didn't budge. "You're right. Serious about their beer security."

"But you've got skills."

"That I do." I grinned and dug into my pocket, pulling out my little lock picking kit. They'd gotten rusty since Venice and needed a workout. "Can't keep these in a dress."

"Certainly not."

Though I had liked wearing it. Just not for work. I glanced around the darkened streets, glad to find it empty. Seemed like we were in a more business-y district or something, since no one was walking from bar to restaurant. "Keep an eye out, okay?"

"Aye." He positioned himself behind me, trying to shield me as I knelt on the cold ground.

I slipped the little picks into the lock and fiddled about, using the skills I'd honed over the years. Finally, there was a click.

"Jackpot." I pulled the picks free and stood.

I yanked open the heavy door, and slipped inside the darkened corridor, Cade at my back.

"Best to do this at night," Cade said.

"No kidding. I'd hate to run into any of those beer-protecting Belgians." I strode silently down the empty hall, seeking an entrance to the tiny harbor that must be inside this building.

It was a simple structure, with wide wood floor planks and white walls that looked to have been added long after the original construction. A light glowed from ahead, and I followed it to a heavy wooden door.

I pressed my ear against the surface, listening. There were no voices, so I slowly pushed it open, peeking inside.

Hundreds of barrels lined the walls, and beyond them, the water glinted darkly. I glanced at Cade and nodded, then slipped inside. He followed, closing the door silently behind him.

We ducked behind some barrels, taking in the room. It was large, probably a third of the size of the whole building.

A man was tying the little boat off to the dock. I waited anxiously as he finished, debating our options.

Finally, I leaned toward Cade and whispered, "I'm going to threaten him into giving us info. Can you glower at him and hit him with your war power? Put the fear of fate into him?"

He nodded.

Good. I didn't relish the idea of scaring the guy, so no way I could actually torture the info out of him. Not even for Rowan. She wouldn't want me to do that to an innocent delivery man.

But that meant we had to make the scaring good.

"On three," I whispered, then counted down.

At three, I slipped out from behind the barrels and silently rushed up to the poor sap, who was now bent over his paperwork and scribbling furiously. He wasn't much bigger than me, so it was easy to wrap an arm around his throat and tug tightly.

A blast of electric energy shot through me, throwing me off

him. I slammed to my back, pain ripping at my insides as confused panic flashed in my mind.

What the hell?

Aching, I scrambled upright in time to see Cade lift the guy off his feet by his lapels, his big hand crushed over the man's mouth to keep him from screaming.

I limped toward them. "What the hell was that?"

Cade glared at the guy and let his magical signature flare. The clashing of swords and the scent of a storm at sea filled the room, along with the silver glow of his aura. He growled, "Answer her. And if you scream, I'll gut you."

The man paled.

Frankly, I might have paled a bit as well. Cade could be damned scary when he wanted to be.

"Well?" Cade's voice was gravel.

The man nodded frantically, his legs twitching in the air.

Cade removed his hand.

"I'm an electric eel shifter." The man gasped. "I do that when I'm startled."

"You're not startled now?" Cade asked.

"Uh, yeah. Wouldn't you be?" Sweat rolled down the man's temple. "But I gotta recharge."

"Then let's make this quick," I said. "And don't stall. Because your puny electric blast can't hurt a guy like my friend here."

The man nodded, eyes wide. "I don't have the keys to the safe, if that's what you want."

"I don't." I leaned close, searching his eyes for truthfulness. "I want to know how you get into the castle. Any passwords when you deliver the beer?" I reached into his front right pocket and removed the wallet that I'd seen peeping out. I pulled an ID card from the thing and read the name, then looked up at him. "Louis?"

"I'll lose my job!" he squeaked.

"You'll lose your life if you don't tell us. And now I know where you live." I waved the card at him as guilt tugged at me. We'd have to make sure he didn't lose his job somehow. But I was willing to deal with that cleanup if it meant rescuing Rowan. "So tell me quick. How do you get in? And don't lie, because I can freaking smell it."

Yeah, that was an actual lie, but I liked the growl in my voice.

His eyes darted, then the words began to spill out. "Bring the boat up to the gate. Press the bow to the metal, then say '*Ik heb een levering voor je van je grootste bewonderaar.*'"

"What does that mean?" I asked, frantically memorizing the phrase.

"I have a delivery from your most fervent admirer. In Dutch. The gate will open. When the guards let you in, don't move quickly. And...."

I poked him in the stomach with my finger. "Tell me."

"If there's another password—sometimes they don't ask for it —it's *Pompoen.*"

"*Pompoen?*"

"Pumpkin in Dutch. I don't know why."

"Fine. Anything else?"

"You don't want to go in there." His eyes were stark. "It's—it's not a good place."

"I don't have a choice. My sister's life is at stake."

"When will the next staff members arrive?" Cade asked.

Sweat rolled down his forehead. "Morning. Maybe eight hours from now."

Cade nodded sharply. "Good. We'll tie you up. They'll find you."

"You're not going to hurt me?"

"Of course not," I said. "We wouldn't be threatening you at all, if it weren't life or death."

The guy nodded, like he got it. Suddenly I felt extra guilty for the scare we'd given him. "Sorry about this."

He didn't forgive me, but he didn't spit on me, either, so I counted it a victory.

Cade lowered him to the ground and found some line to bind his hands and wrists, then he set him up in a chair near some barrels.

Before he could bind the guy's mouth, our captive spoke. "If you're going tonight, tell them you have the *Tripel*."

"The beer?"

"Yes. The Viscount wanted more of it. Maybe it will make you less suspicious to them."

My chest warmed. "Thanks."

"For your sister. I wouldn't want anyone to be trapped in that castle. But just—just bring my boat back if you can."

I looked at Cade, really wanting to fulfill the guy's request but knowing we probably couldn't.

Cade's brow wrinkled. "We'll bring you a replacement if we can't get this one."

The man's shoulders slumped.

"We'll try," I promised. "We'll make this right."

Cade bound the man's mouth quickly. While he worked, I scouted the barrels for a few that said TRIPEL. I spotted them close by and gestured Cade to follow me.

"Let's load a couple of these. Make it look real."

"Get the empties off the boat. I'll bring these."

I did as he asked, heaving three empty barrels off the boat so he could replace them with full ones. Then we climbed on the boat and undid the lines. The engine hummed quietly as we started it up, and I took one last look at the guy we'd just screwed.

I wanted to say sorry again, but it was more for my benefit than his, so I kept my mouth shut.

Rowan, I reminded myself. *Rowan.*

Cade drove us down the river back to the castle. As we neared, I called upon my magic from Loki, building an illusion that made Cade look like the beer delivery man and made me disappear into thin air.

"Well done." Cade maneuvered the boat up to the gate and pressed the bow to it. "*Ik heb een levering voor je van je grootste bewonderaar.*"

Man, this Viscount guy had to be totally full of himself.

"Wat is er?" a voice barked.

Cade glanced at me. He couldn't see me, but I'd bet my eyes were as wide as his right now. We didn't know Dutch.

"Shit," I murmured.

"*Tripel.*" Cade said, trying to pitch his voice to that of the delivery guy's. "*Tripel.*"

There was a smattering of Dutch, no doubt the guards debating. My heart leapt into my throat as I waited.

Come on. Come on.

Finally, the gate creaked slowly open.

Yes.

I stayed stock-still as Cade drove the boat through the gate, trying not to move a single muscle. Trying not to even breathe.

It was damp and dark within the castle's tiny underground harbor. A demon stood on a narrow walkway next to a gate, glaring at us. His horns were sawed off, and his vest was hung with wicked-looking blades.

I wanted to hit him with a dagger right off the bat, but what if there were a lot more of them? Or another checkpoint?

Better to play by their rules.

"Paswoord?" he growled.

The question didn't sound like the last one. So the answer couldn't be *Tripel.*

Jeez, looked like I needed to study languages *and* learn to walk in high heels if I really wanted to be successful at the Protectorate. This undercover spy stuff was hard. Even looking like the delivery guy didn't assuage this guard's suspicion.

Cade's brow wrinkled briefly, then he said, "*Pompoen.*"

The guard frowned, then nodded, gesturing ahead of us.

My shoulders sagged.

Thank fates.

Cade steered the boat slowly toward the wider part of the tiny harbor. The guard ambled along beside us, eyeing the contents of the boat. Good thing we'd put the *Tripel* barrels in.

Cade pulled the boat up to the dock, where two more demons waited. Same species, all with sawed-off horns and magic that smelled like mold. Or maybe it was this dank underground cave built of stone and filled with gross water.

As Cade tied the boat off, I laid my hand on his back and leaned near to his ear, close enough to breathe, "Now."

I lunged up, drew my daggers from the ether, and hurled them at the two farthest guards. The blades shined as they turned end over end, finally sinking into the necks of the demons. Chests were bigger targets, but with demons, you never could quite tell where the heart was located.

But everyone needed their necks.

Blood spurted from around the blades as the demons grabbed at their necks, eyes wide. They tumbled onto their backs, landing with a thud.

Beside me, Cade drew his sword from the ether and lunged toward the last remaining demon, swinging gracefully. He decapitated the beast before it could draw its own weapon, and I dodged an arc of arterial blood.

When the demon fell and the blood stopped spraying, I straightened. "Well, that's our good deed for the day. Sending those bastards back where they belong."

"They'll be back again, eventually."

"True enough." I hopped out onto the stone quay.

It didn't take demons terribly long to wake up in the under-world once their bodies had disappeared from Earth. But getting out was often harder, requiring dark magic that was most frequently sponsored by some lowlife scum like the Viscount.

I didn't like to throw around the phrase "low-life scum," but the guy had a torture dungeon. That was enough for me.

Cade followed me off the boat, and we began to search the underground harbor. There wasn't much. Just a stone quay wedged between the murky water and a wall. One door clearly led up into the castle, but a few more went to mysterious places.

"Where the hell is the waterfall?" Cade asked.

I studied the dingy water that our boat floated upon. It looked still, but the boat was being dragged slightly to the back of the harbor, which was a dead-end. The motor was off, so how was that possible? I peered hard at the water. Just barely, I could make out the movement of the murky stuff.

Jackpot.

I pointed toward the back wall. "Some of the water is headed that way. The boat is tugging at the lines."

"You think some of the water is flowing out and going down into the earth? Under the castle, like a waterfall?"

"Yep. So we need to go deeper into the castle."

"Let's find out which door conceals our prize."

I headed straight for the door closest to the back of the harbor, which was where I hoped the waterfall was located. When I pressed my ear to the wood and used Heimdall's power, I picked up the sound of trickling water. "Let's try this one."

I tugged at the door, but it wouldn't budge. The door handle felt weirdly sticky beneath my palm, and I drew away, inspecting it. "Ew. Spiderwebs."

I tried to shake it off my hand—an instinctual freak-out reaction that obviously did no good—then rubbed my palm against the rough stone wall.

"Looks like they don't use this often, then."

"Try never."

Cade grinned and tugged open the door, putting his strength into it until the lock broke and the door swung open.

"That works," I said, staring down the dark spiral staircase leading down. A sickly yellow light glowed from below. "Right out of a ghost story."

"I'm telling you, this place is creepy."

I stepped into the hall. "Don't worry, hon. I'll protect you."

He pressed a kiss to the back of my head. "I'm counting on it."

I grinned, liking his slightly teasing tone. It was playful, but also like he really might trust me to do it. And couldn't I? My new powers were making me mega capable. And he'd always *been* mega capable.

So we'd protect each other.

Yep. I liked that idea.

Cade quietly shut the door behind us, and I made my way down the stairs, my steps silent and all my senses alert. A faint glow came from below, the only illumination in the dark, damp stairwell. My improved eyesight probably helped, because light couldn't have an easy time traveling up a spiral staircase.

This was the worst part of castles—the cold reality of ancient stones and dampness. I dragged my fingertips along the walls, steadying myself as I tried not to lose my footing on the tiny stairs.

The glow grew brighter, bluer and fiercer, bringing with it a clammy feeling and a dusty scent.

"Do you feel that?" Cade murmured from behind me.

"Yeah." I shuddered. "Feels awful."

Whatever this magic was, I wouldn't like it.

As the light shined brighter on the walls, I noticed the deep scratch marks in the stone. *Creepy.*

By the time we reached a small landing that glowed with a bright blue light, the dark magic had made me queasy. My heart thundered and my stomach turned.

The space was small. Eight feet by six feet, max, and a glowing blue wall blocked our way. It was semi-transparent, but hard to see through. The magic that emitted from it made my skin crawl and my muscles weaken.

"What the hell is it?" I asked.

Cade stepped closer to me, gripping my hand. His warmth flowed up my arm, strengthening my muscles. I still wouldn't stand a chance in a fight—not with this weird magic affecting me—but he made me feel better.

And not just because it was him. Because he was *alive* and that wall felt like death.

Cade leaned in front of me, reaching for the stone wall at my right. He pulled a clump of strange yellow moss off the rock— how the hell did it live in this kind of environment?—and tossed it at the shimmering blue wall.

The moss sailed through, crumbling into brown dust as the light surrounded it.

"The wall is death," Cade said. "An ancient magic. One that cannot be manipulated by humans."

"So we can't cross it?" Panic welled in my chest, my gaze riveted to the crumbled brown moss that was turning to dust.

I'd die for Rowan. For Ana.

No question.

But if I died *before* I got the antidote to the spell? That'd be pointless. My mind scrambled.

How the hell could we pass through this wall? I studied it, taking in everything, hunting for an idea. *Anything.*

When the wall in front of me shimmered, I almost didn't notice.

Cade squeezed my hand. "Look."

My gaze darted toward it.

A figure stepped out of the shimmering blue. It was made of the same blue light, but a haze of gray surrounded it. A cowl covered its features, long robes dusting the floor. As it drifted nearer to us, I flinched, stepping backward.

It reminded me of a Phantom, but this creature was *death*. Far worse than any Phantom.

"Stop!" I commanded.

I couldn't fight this thing, and I didn't want to run. Not when we were so close.

The creature didn't stop. I drew my blade from the ether and pointed it toward the figure. The feeling of death closed over me, a darkness that seeped through my muscles and tried to drag me to the floor.

The figure's chest pierced itself on my blade, but it didn't seem to notice. My muscles tensed. I stepped backward, but the creature drifted to a stop, my blade still piercing its chest.

"You dare to trespass upon my domain?" Its voice sounded like the winds of death.

"I'd prefer not to, honestly," I said.

"We seek a flower," Cade said. "A single bloom."

"A bloom with more magic than you can comprehend," the creature hissed.

"Well, that's why we want it," Cade said. "We must pass."

"Perhaps you might."

"Are you death?" I asked.

"I am not, but I am his minion."

That wasn't much better. "How do we cross?"

"Seven seconds to answer a riddle. Do not fail, or you shall fall. The kiss of death I shall place upon thee."

I shivered, colder than I'd ever been in all my life.

If this creature lunged for us, I couldn't escape. Its magic had weakened me too greatly. And if it touched me...

Death.

No question.

"What's the riddle?" Cade asked.

The creature hissed, soft and fast,

"As I was going to St. Ives,

I met a man with seven wives,

Each wife had seven sacks,

Each sack had seven cats,

Each cat had seven kits:

Kits, cats, sacks, and wives,

How many were there going to St. Ives?"

Oh shit—math.

My mind raced. Seven times seven times seven times seven. Or was it plus seven?

A noise buzzed in my head as I tried to calculate how many there were. Beside me, Cade murmured softly. Quickly.

Come on. Come on.

I tried to recite it again in my head. Had I missed something? *As I was going to St. Ives.*

It pinged in my head. This wasn't a math problem at all. It was a freaking riddle.

I looked up at Cade. His eyes were wide as they met mine, sudden understanding dawning in their green depths.

"One." We said it at the same time, then turned to death's minion. "One."

"It's just one," I said. "Only he is going to St. Ives. The others don't go with him. He meets them on the way, so they're going the *other* direction."

Death's minion inclined his head, then swept his arm out to

the blue wall. The terrible magic shimmered and disappeared, along with death's minion.

"Oh shit." A shuddery breath escaped me, and I raced through, sparing a glance for the crumbled brown remains of the moss.

Sweat dampened my skin as I continued hurrying down the stairs, finally spilling out onto a narrow platform at the edge of a great cavern. I teetered on the edge of a cliff that plunged downward, arms pinwheeling and the sword in my hand glinting in the light from above.

Cade grabbed the back of my shirt and yanked me back. I collapsed against the wall next to him, panting.

"This place is incredible," Cade said.

"No kidding."

The sight before me was stunning. It was massive, a huge domed cavern that glowed with light emitting from large shining rocks in the ceiling. A ledge ran high along the wall, circling around the cavern to the far side, where it spilled water in a thin waterfall. The water glowed clear and light blue, almost like the muddy river water had been filtered through the earth before being poured into a pool.

I pointed to it. "It must flow from the river above, around the cavern, and then spill into there."

"Not easy to get there, though."

"No, it's not." We were a good hundred yards away, and there was a massive crevasse in the ground in front of us. It stretched twenty yards, with spindly spires of stone sticking up to form a hopscotch of a bridge. On the other side, a field of flowers sat sandwiched between the crevasse and the pool of water.

I crept toward the edge and peered down into the blackness. I could fly across, but Cade...

He stepped up beside me. "You fly. I'll walk."

"No. Too dangerous."

"This is nothing."

Dark magic shimmered up from the depths. "Let me test it. This doesn't feel right. After death's minion tried to stop us, no way this will be easy."

Cade frowned, brow creased.

I called on my wings, letting them flare behind my back. I pointed to them. "Let me test it. These will protect me. Falling won't be an issue."

He nodded, and though he clearly didn't like me testing the dangerous stuff, he wasn't dumb enough to tell me not to. And he trusted me.

I liked that.

I sucked in a breath and gripped my sword—my security blanket—then stepped onto the first stone. It was only about a foot in diameter, and who knew how tall it was.

I certainly didn't want to find out.

My heart thundered as I hopped from stone to stone. I was ten feet from the edge when it crumbled beneath my feet. I plummeted, a scream trapped in my throat and my stomach jumping.

I nearly dropped my sword from the shock, but I gripped it tightly. My wings caught the air, and I forced them down, flying upward.

Something grabbed my ankle.

I kicked and looked down. A dark gray vine twined around my ankle, pulling me down.

"Bree!" Cade shouted, fear in his voice.

I doubled over, swinging my sword downward to sever the vine. My steel clashed with it, but bounced off, as if the thing were made of impenetrable rubber.

Oh, shit.

10

My head roared as the vine dragged me down. No matter how hard I moved my wings, I wasn't strong enough. My heart drummed against my ribs.

A flash of ghostly blue shined in the corner of my vision. It darted down toward the vine.

Mayhem!

She blasted her flame at the vine, a massive plume bigger than any she'd ever created. The vine recoiled, releasing my ankle and jerking away.

I shot into the air, flying high over the crevasse and toward the waterfall. When I'd cleared the dangerous gorge, I landed at a run, panting. I finally found my footing and spun to check on Mayhem.

She was fluttering high up, a pleased grin on her face, but it was Cade who caught my eye.

He was scaling the far wall, descending into the crevasse to rescue me. He was going to go down, across, and up. And damn, he was fast.

"Cade! Stop!"

He halted and turned. Relief flashed on his face when he

saw me, and he hurriedly began to climb back up. A whip of dark gray vine extended up from below him.

"Mayhem!" I pointed to the vine.

She flashed toward it, blowing her flame at the vine and escorting Cade up to the top.

"Thanks for trying!" I shouted at him, really quite thrilled that he kept leaping into danger for me. Not that I wanted him to get hurt trying to save me—hell no—but the idea that he would? Repeatedly?

Yeah, I liked that a *lot.*

I shook the thoughts away and turned. We didn't have a lot of time, and I needed that damned flower. At least the Rebel Gods needed Rowan for her magic. That would keep her alive. I hoped.

A field of flowers spread in front of me, in every shade from the rainbow glinting in the strange white light from overhead.

"Ah, crap." It was a lot of flowers.

And they all looked different.

Like, whoa different.

This would take *hours.*

I called upon Heimdall's magic, hoping to strengthen my vision to be able to spot the red flower with the dripping petals. It worked, but I still had to sort through them all, gazing at each one for at least a half second.

Slowly, I walked through the flowers, anxiety rising with every step. What if it wasn't here?

I sucked in a calming breath and kept going.

After ten minutes with no luck, I groaned and dragged my fingers through my hair. This wasn't working. There were just too many.

I spun in a circle, eyeing the whole place.

A flower with dripping petals...

My eye caught on the waterfall.

Duh.

I hurried toward the spilling water, edging around the pool and climbing over rocks to reach the falls. The water glowed with an eerie white light, sparkling as I neared.

Maybe the water was what helped the flower become so powerful?

Droplets splashed my face as I neared, refreshing and crisp. They fizzed, like champagne pops on the tongue. I folded my wings into my body, slipping behind the falls into an alcove. The small space glittered with light from more of the strange stones that were in the ceiling. They shined on the ground, illuminating a single flower.

A red flower with a purple center—dripping water from the petals.

Joy burst in my chest, a buzz that sang through my whole body.

Shaking, I dug the hard, plastic container out of my pocket and unscrewed the lid. Water soaked through my jeans as I knelt and picked the small bloom, placing it carefully inside the container and screwing the lid back on.

I tucked it back in my jacket pocket and zipped it up to keep the flower safe. It took some wiggling of the zipper to make it fit, but I managed.

As soon as it was safe, I sprinted from behind the waterfall and raced through the field of flowers. Cade waited for me on the other side, a grin stretched across his face.

"You found it?"

He didn't have to shout, and he knew it. My new hearing picked it up. I nodded enthusiastically and unfurled my wings, taking off into the air and flying high over the crevasse. I eyed it for more of the dark gray vines, but Mayhem flew below me, a furry escort with breath of fire.

I was panting as I landed, excitement racing through me. "Let's get out of here."

Cade nodded and turned, expression now businesslike. As he started up the stairs, I grabbed his arm. "Slowly. Just in case that death wall pops back up."

Fortunately, it didn't. But by the time we made it up to the main level, I could hear commotion in the tiny harbor. I tugged on the back of Cade's shirt, but he'd already stopped.

"You hear that?" I whispered.

"Aye. My wolf gives me better hearing. Sounds like they've found the boat. And noticed the missing guards."

I nodded. The demons' bodies would have disappeared by now, returned to their underworld.

"I'll make us invisible."

"Aye, good plan. But we'll need to go out another way. We won't be able to get through the enchanted gate."

I stuck out my hand. "Hang on to me, then, and let's find another way out."

He grinned, a devastating sight, and took my hand.

A frisson raced up my arm, and I shivered.

Shaking away any distraction, I called upon Loki's magic, imagining us becoming invisible. It raced over me, cool and bright, and Cade disappeared in front of my eyes.

He tugged on my hand, and I followed, keeping my footsteps silent. We paused at the door, and it slowly swung open an inch.

Cade must be peering out.

After a moment, he tugged harder on my hand, and I swiftly followed him out of the stairwell, trying not to bump into him.

The stone platform in the harbor bustled with guards, all of whom were facing away at that moment. Four demons were inspecting the boat, while another was shining a light onto the water.

Carefully, I shut the door behind me.

Not a moment too soon.

I turned to see a demon facing us, his gaze sweeping over the door. I stood stock-still, heart thundering, praying that he wasn't a species with great hearing or sense of smell. He had dark green skin and yellow eyes, a breed I'd never seen before.

He began to approach.

Cade pulled my hand, and I followed, chafing slightly at him being in the lead. But we'd started it this way, trapped in the narrow stairwell, and I didn't want to switch anything up. The two of us jockeying for power was dumb.

I might hate not being able to make my own moves, but if I was going to give someone else control, he was the only one I could tolerate. Besides Ana and Rowan.

We strode silently toward the only open door in the room, passing the demon with only a few feet to spare. His nose twitched briefly, but he kept going.

As we finally slipped through the open doorway and made our way up the stairs, my heart was pounding so loudly it would give me a headache later.

After so much time spent in Death Valley, I hated feeling trapped. And this hulking castle definitely qualified as a trap.

The stairway led into a hallway that reminded me a lot of the older section of the Protectorate castle. Heavy stones made up the floor and wall, while flickering sconces shed a golden light on the walls.

We leaned against the wall and took stock of our surroundings. There were no doors save for the heavy wooden ones at either end of the hall.

At times like these, I wished I had Cass's dragon sense to lead me out of here.

"We're still fairly low," Cade said. "The basement, I think. We need to find our way up to the castle wall."

"The gates will probably be pretty fierce there as well."

"You can fly."

"Yeah, but you can't."

"I can jump. My wolf is not...normal."

"I'll say. Those walls looked to be thirty feet high."

"It's nothing."

I couldn't see him, but I could hear his grin. "All right, then. Let's make it to the top." I turned left, figuring that door was as good as any other, and kept the illusion of invisibility going as we made our way down the hall, our steps silent and in sync.

We stopped in front of the door.

"Ready?" I whispered.

Cade squeezed my hand in affirmation, and I opened the door.

The interior was dark as pitch, but I stepped in anyway. Cade followed. I blinked as I tried to adjust my vision, but even Heimdall's magic couldn't help me see through this inky blackness.

I stepped forward tentatively, and the smell that rolled toward me made me gag. Old blood and...

Ugh.

I couldn't tell what. But I didn't like it.

I spun, dragging Cade with me, determined to get out of this hellhole.

The door slammed. My heart leapt into my throat. I drew my sword from the ether as the lights flared on.

It was just a flickering flame, but after the pitch darkness, it was as bright as the sun. I turned back, Cade still gripping my hand. I couldn't see him, but I could feel that he, too, had his sword drawn.

A man stood across from us, slight and pale. Long white hair hung around his cadaverous face, and the light that burned from his white eyes was pure evil.

The furnishings in the room drew my attention. They were

massive, hulking things, and horror dawned on me as I looked closer.

Torture chamber.

This wasn't furniture. And this wasn't a normal room.

And this dude...

He seriously was *not* normal.

I swallowed hard, quietly stepping backward and thanking Loki for the power of invisibility.

"Ah, ah, ah. Don't go so fast." His voice creaked like an old rocking chair, but there was nothing comforting about it.

Could he see us?

"Of course I can see you. Or rather, I can sense you. Your life force." His voice shivered with anticipation and I gagged. "I'd like to take it from you. Slowly."

Oh, screw this.

I darted for the door, dragging Cade behind me. He didn't hesitate. Normally, we'd fight.

But this dude...

He couldn't be fought. I could just tell.

My hand was around the door handle when something cold and wet exploded against my back. My whole body froze solid. Cade's hand went stiff in my own.

"What the hell?!" It took me a moment to realize that I'd screamed in my mind, not out loud. I *couldn't* scream out loud.

Potion bomb.

I thrashed, trying to break free of the magic that held me frozen, but my muscles stayed stiff. Solid. I was a human two-by-four, with as much mobility.

The bastard had frozen us solid.

"It's been so long since I've had visitors." His voice came from nearby, but all I could see was the damned door.

Visions of the torture devices were burned into my mind,

however. Strange benches and vises and metal things that made no sense.

My skin chilled with fear as breath wafted over my neck.

It smelled of dust and death.

Was this guy even alive?

He hadn't looked alive.

"Now what should I do with you?" he hissed.

I shuddered inside, the rest of me frozen. No matter how I struggled, this monster's power kept me frozen. Cade was silent next to me, unable to talk. But his energy flared, his magical signature bombarding me.

He was fighting this.

Of course he was.

The monster pinched my side. I tried to flinch away, to gag. But I couldn't even move.

The freezing spell is so damned strong.

Tears burned my eyes, unable to fall. I couldn't fight. I couldn't leap into action.

I was *trapped.*

With Rowan's antidote in my damned pocket.

My muscles burned with pain as I fought the freezing charm.

Motion exploded next to me. Cade's hand yanked away from mine. A shriek sounded from behind me, and the magic that bound me snapped apart.

I gasped and swung around, dropping the invisibility magic.

Cade had thrown the man across the room, but he rose like a spider. One arm dangled at his side, but he didn't seem to notice.

"Zombie," Cade muttered.

Ah shit. It was hard to kill a zombie.

Cade lunged for it, moving so quickly that he was nearly a blur. He severed both arms and legs, then went for the head.

The creature was in pieces moments later, and I sagged with relief.

"Who's ever heard of a zombie torture master?"

"I don't know how this one kept his wits long enough to become a master of anything. Even torture."

I shook my head. "No idea."

On the floor, the arms crawled back to the body. The legs followed, drawn by the dark magic that still stank like death and dust. Finally, the head rolled against the stone ground.

It was literally the worst thing I'd ever seen.

As soon as it attached to the body, the creature leapt up, grin firmly in place.

I swallowed hard, skin chilled.

"So, we can't kill it." I raised my sword. My gaze darted around, searching for anything.

A large cage in the corner—I *so* did not want to think about its former use—caught my eye. I pointed. "There!"

"Got it."

Cade raised his sword again, decapitating the zombie once more.

The beast was still fast, despite its lack of head. Cade dismembered the creature so fast that it didn't have time to get its claws into him.

"Quick!" he said.

I stashed my sword in the ether and grimaced as I bent to pick up the two arms. They felt awful. Squishy yet firm.

Ugh, ugh, ugh.

I sprinted for the cage, heart thundering.

The fingers wiggled and clawed for me. "Oh, this is *the worst.*"

I reached the cage and dropped the arms, then yanked the door open and kicked them inside before turning to Cade.

He ran toward me, the head and torso in his arms. A grimace

of disgust twisted his features, and he threw them into the cage like a morbid baseball player, not even waiting to reach the entrance.

"Get the others." I pointed to the legs. "I'm on door duty."

A brief grin sliced through his grimace, and he wheeled, making quick work of tossing the legs into the cage.

I slammed the door shut and turned to him. "You took the head."

"Aye."

"You are literally the greatest guy I have ever known."

His right brow quirked. "For making it so that you didn't have to carry a decapitated zombie head?"

"I have my priorities." I swung my arms around his neck and kissed him hard on the mouth, then pulled away.

There was no time to linger, but joy over what we had glowed inside me.

Sure, this wasn't a normal relationship. But you really got to know a person when fighting for your lives. And he was good and kind and strong.

And he carried the zombie head so I didn't have to.

The perfect man.

And I might want a real date one day. But until then....

This was good.

As long as we survived and got out of this creepy place.

A scraping noise from behind me indicated that the zombie was starting to piece itself together. Since I didn't want to see it clawing at the cage walls, I tugged on Cade. "Let's find a way out."

"Couldn't do it soon enough."

Fortunately, there was an exit on the other side of the room, away from the door we'd entered through. Dimly lit stairs led up to another level. We stopped at the closed door and listened.

"Coast sounds clear," I murmured.

Cade nodded. I reached out my hand. He took it, and I turned us invisible.

We stepped out into the hallway, which was slightly more modern. The floors were wood instead of stone, and the lights electric. Some kind of old-timey sconce style, but they'd at least attempted to modernize the living spaces in the castle.

Both directions down the hall looked the same, so I went right. We wove our way silently through the castle, seeking an exit.

This place was *big*.

And fairly empty, besides the guards down below. And the creepy torture zombie. I shuddered at the thought.

Would the Viscount be mad that we'd locked up his monster? Or did he even know that thing was down there?

We stepped out into a large, empty room. The ceiling soared far overhead, and over a dozen chandeliers dripped sparkling crystal drops. On the far side, a throne sat against the wall. It was a massive golden thing that dwarfed the man within.

The Viscount?

What the heck was he doing, sitting here all alone?

It reminded me of *Great Expectations*, actually.

I glanced at Cade before remembering that I couldn't see him. As much as I wanted to investigate, my priority was Rowan.

I hurried toward the exit on the side wall.

"Who goes there?" The Viscount's voice cracked down the hall.

I glanced toward him, startled. Our footsteps had been silent, and the invisibility was working. Though I didn't know what type of supernatural he was, I put money on something with great hearing or smell.

We picked up the pace, silently running toward the exit.

"Guards!" the Viscount roared. "Dogs!"

Oh shit!

Dogs definitely had a great sense of smell.

I broke into a full-out sprint, Cade at my side. Didn't matter if they could hear us if there were freaking dogs.

We spilled out into a foyer, then shot for the large double doors. Two guards stood in front of them, their beefy arms crossed over their chests. Their eyes widened as they heard our footsteps approach, and they drew their wickedly sharp blades.

Cade's hand yanked away from mine, and his footsteps thundered louder ahead of me.

The guards lifted up into the air and flew aside.

He'd thrown them!

The doors burst open.

I raced out into the night, my lungs burning. As soon as I hit the open courtyard, I unfurled my wings and took off into the sky. Behind me, dogs barked, their feet pounding on the ground as they sprinted across the yard toward us. Wind tore at my hair, excitement bursting through me.

Sure, we were running for our lives. But flying was fun.

Flying while escaping with a cure for my sister? That was double fun.

I soared over the large castle walls, the city and river spread out around me. I spun on the air, searching behind me. After a few seconds, I dropped the illusion of invisibility. I had to see Cade—had to see if he needed my help making it over the wall.

A wolf appeared in midair, flying over the high castle wall.

Holy crap, he could jump.

He sailed down onto the lawn below, landing in a crouch, then stood and shifted back to human.

Man, he was no ordinary wolf shifter. God powers were badass.

I dropped to the ground next to him and folded my wings back into my body. It was the coolest trick, allowing me to look totally normal out in the real world. And to sleep well, since sleeping on wings would suck.

"Good work." I panted. "Let's get to the drop point."

Cade grinned and nodded. I spun and raced off, him at my side. We sprinted down the city streets, leaving the castle and its creepy denizens behind.

It didn't take long for us to reach our bags, and Cade called the Protectorate. A minute later, Emily and Ana showed up.

"She insisted on coming," Emily said.

"Did you get it?" Ana demanded.

"I did. Let's go. Can you take us straight to Hedy's workshop?"

"Sure thing," Emily said.

Ana grabbed Emily's shoulder, and the dark-haired girl reached for my hand. I took it. Cade took her other, and she transported us all back to the Protectorate castle.

The night was cool and the moon large, gleaming on the castle. The windows shined golden and bright, a welcome home that I would never get sick of.

This place really was our home now, and I couldn't wait to bring Rowan here.

Sure, I needed to finish at the Academy, but I'd do anything to make that happen. Because this place, and these people, were what I wanted more than anything.

Rowan would be the icing on the cake.

I turned to Emily. "Thank you for getting us."

"Of course. Resident taxi." She grinned. "At least when transportation charms are low."

"Could you do us a favor?" Cade asked. "We stole a barge from the *Zwarte Kat* brewery. And left a nice kid locked up in their wharf. Could you find a way to replace his boat and untie him?"

"Tonight, if possible," I added. "I know it's a tall order, but he wasn't a bad guy. I don't want him to lose his job."

She smiled. "I like a challenge. I'll see what I can do. The Protectorate has some contacts."

"You're the best." I really needed to get to know her better. Maybe I was high on the victory of finding the flower and everything was sappy, but I was loving this place right now.

Finally, things felt really possible. Rowan was alive, and I had the antidote to the curse that bound her to Cocidius and stole her mind.

"Let's get this potion made," Ana said.

"I thought that Mordaca said you could make it yourself?" Cade said. "Just mix with water and boil?"

Ana laughed. "Sure, if I trusted myself. Or her." She nodded toward me.

I grinned. "Let's get an expert to do it. The potion may only require water, but I'm not taking any risks."

We knocked on the door to Hedy's tower. I'd never noticed before, but the door was a beautiful thing, featuring a tree carved out of golden wood.

"Coming!" Hedy's voice sounded from the mullioned glass window above.

Footsteps thudded on the stairs inside—I really needed to learn how to turn off Heimdall's power—and the door swung open a moment later.

"Did you get it?" Hedy's eyes were bright and her lavender hair messy. Her silver robe was as slick as melted metal.

"I did."

Her lips split into a smile. "Come in, come in. I'll call Jude to get an update on the others."

I prayed they'd found Chernobog's realm. With the cure and directions to both of the other gods' realms, we were almost there.

We followed Hedy inside as she placed a quick call. I dug the flower out of my pocket and put it on her worktable. A warm orange lamp glowed from the middle of the ceiling, illuminating the cluttered space that was filled with the tools of Hedy's magic.

She lowered her phone and turned. "Jude says Ali and Haris think they are close. Cass is helping them. They'll be back in the morning, hopefully."

"Perfect." I pointed to the potion. "Can you make that into the cure for Rowan? Mordaca said to just mix it with water and boil."

Hedy nodded. "I spoke to her about it. It will only take a moment."

She got to work, and we watched silently.

Ana leaned her shoulder against mine. "It's finally happening."

"I know." Tears pricked my eyes, and I squeezed Ana's hand. "We still have to find her. But we're so close."

"Just two realms to check."

"If only we could just freaking *ask* her where she was." I'd never been a fan of cell phones—not much use for them in our old life—but now, I'd kill to be able to ring her up and say, "Hey, where you at? I'll come get you."

Sure, it'd take an army and a lot of offensive magic to get her, but we had that. All we needed was a *place.*

Hedy turned to us, brows drawn. "Ask her where she is?"

"Yeah."

She nodded, the wheels clearly turning in her head. "Do you still have any of her hair?"

I glanced at Ana, startled, then back at Hedy. "Yeah, we do."

"I might be able to help. There's a spell that uses a mirror and something from the person you want to contact. You'll have one shot."

"Anything." My heart leapt.

"We'll have to be careful, though," Ana said. "She goes in and out of the enchantment. If we get her at the wrong time, she might alert Cocidius or the other gods that we're coming for her."

"Could we just spy on her?" I asked. "Never let her know we're looking?"

Cade smiled at me. "That could work well."

"Yes," Hedy said. "If you're silent, and in a dark place, she may not even notice you are watching. But the mirror will only work once."

"We'll take what we can get. Thank you."

"Of course. You're one of us." She handed me the completed vial of antidote. It was ruby red with swirls of purple. "One dose. She must drink. And get me the last strands of her hair. Along with some of your own."

I took the vial with a grateful nod, then yanked out a few long hairs and handed them over. Ana did the same. "I'll get you the rest of Rowan's hairs. They're in my room."

"I'll have the mirror done for you by early tomorrow morning," Hedy said. "You can pick it up before you go after Rowan. Hopefully Ali and Haris will have had luck with Cass."

I freaking hoped so. It was the last piece of the puzzle, and we really needed it to fall into place.

11

Cade and I walked out of Hedy's place with Ana. She sprinted off toward the castle, determined to get Hedy the key ingredient for the mirror, but Cade and I lingered.

"I need to head back to my place soon," he said. "But I'll be here early in the morning. As soon as Ali and Haris give us what they know, we'll set off. We'll find Rowan, Bree. I promise."

I squeezed him tight, leaning my head against his chest. "Thank you for being by my side through all this."

We'd just kind of fallen into a natural rhythm, the two of us, doing what we did best. Kicking ass, mostly. And I liked it.

I leaned back. "I think I'm starting to like you."

"Just starting?" His lips kicked up at the corner, a devastatingly sexy grin that made my head spin.

"Maybe it started a little while ago. But now I'm positive. I definitely like you."

"So you'd say yes to a date when this is all over? A real one?"

"Something that's not running for our lives or drinking beer at the Whisky and Warlock?"

"I was thinking more along the lines of long walks on the

beach, riding a tandem bike, gazing at the sunset...." He had the tone of one of those old dating shows.

I laughed.

He shook his head. "I quite like the Whisky and Warlock, but no. I was thinking of something that would put you back into Caro's dress."

"So that you can take me out of it?" I grinned cheekily.

"I make no assumptions." He sounded like an angel. Totally pure. And maybe a little full of it.

"I'd like that. A lot." I leaned up and kissed him, falling briefly into the magical sensation of his lips against mine.

A blast of warmth hit my cheek, and I jerked back. Mayhem was floating nearby, a ham in her mouth.

"Party pooper," I said.

She flew in a loop-de-loop, then farted a poof of fire.

I laughed and looked at Cade. "That's my cue. I need to rest up. Can't be low on power tomorrow."

"No. We have important work to do."

Did we ever.

The next morning, I woke with the dawn, throwing on clothes and zipping the antidote into the pocket of my jacket.

Mayhem and Chaos were conked out on my couch, but Ruckus was nowhere to be seen. Off causing mischief, no doubt. But I definitely didn't have time to worry about it.

I hurried out of my tower apartment and into the hall, meeting Ana as she left her own door.

"Hey. Did you get the mirror?" I asked.

"Yep. I snuck down there before dawn to get it."

"Perfect. I hope it works."

"Same."

We rushed through the hall and down to the main foyer, heading to the kitchen to grab a quick breakfast before meeting with everyone in the round room.

We had just stepped back into the foyer, our bellies full, when the front door of the castle burst open. Ali, Haris, and Cass spilled in, their hair windblown and cheeks red. Caro followed behind. Her silver eyes sparkled with excitement.

"Did you find it?" I asked.

"We did," Ali said.

"With some help." Cass stepped aside.

A tall, slender man entered behind her. He glowed a pale golden color, his simple trousers and shirt looking like they were spun from watery sunlight.

The magic that flowed from him made me gasp. The strength of it made me stumble briefly. Was he a god? It felt like a warm summer day, and smelled of fresh grass and cool water.

"I am Belobog." His voice had the hum of a breeze.

"Slavic god of sunshine and life," Cass said.

With magic that felt like this, he had to be a good guy, then. I smiled. "Nice to meet you."

"I've come to assist you with Chernobog." Besides having a nice voice, he spoke in a stilted style that was somewhat strange. Probably didn't get out much.

"Thank you," Ana said. "We'll take all the help we can get."

"Let's go to the round room," I said. "The others are waiting."

"Are you hungry?" Ana asked. "You've been gone all night."

Dang. Points to Ana for being good.

"Actually, we're great!" Haris said. "Belobog gave us a little burst of his light, and I'm totally refreshed."

I raised a brow. These guys could always eat something, so Belobog's power had to be something.

"Good. Let's go." I turned and led the group toward the

round room, falling back to thank Cass. "I really appreciate you working nonstop to find my sister."

"Of course." She tucked her red hair behind her ear. "You helped us a lot, years ago. We're just sorry we couldn't find her sooner. But having so many people tracking them has made it easier. It's hard for a god to hide his magic."

"So you really found the entrance to Chernobog's realm?"

"According to Belobog, yes. But it will take some effort to get to."

When we were this close to saving Rowan, there was no amount of effort that would keep me from her.

Everyone gathered around the big table in the round room, joining Jude and Hedy. We fell right into discussion, Belobog leading the way.

Stilted speech or no, he was comfortable with his godly power. "Your friend here found me while they were searching for Chernobog's lair in Germany. Near the Baltic. He has been a plague on the region, one that I have been unable to fight."

"We'll help you," Cade said.

Belobog inclined his head. "Thank you. That is what your friends said. If you can get rid of Chernobog, it will do the world much good."

"What's he doing that is such a scourge?" I asked.

"I am light, and Chernobog is darkness. I am life, and he is death. Illness. Once, we were in harmony. Each with power, neither good nor bad. One required for the other." He shook his head. "But long ago, he fell into alliance with the Rebel Gods. He wanted more than his half of the day. More than his half of existence. They've given it to him. And as a result, his dark realm has spilled out onto the earth, polluting a small section of the coast in northern Germany."

"It's a flipping nightmare, all right." Ali leaned back in his chair, dark eyes and hair gleaming. He was wearing another soccer jersey—or football, as he insisted on calling it. He didn't seem to have an alliance to any team, just the style.

"Dark, depressing. Dangerous," Haris said.

"We didn't go all the way through," Cass said. "It was too far. Miles. But I know that the entrance to Chernobog's lair is within the polluted area. By the coast. I could feel it."

"How many miles?" I asked Belobog. I just couldn't wait any longer, to be honest.

"Twenty miles, perhaps a bit more. It's been a long time since I've made it out to the sea. His magic has polluted it for far too long, making travel difficult."

I looked at Ana, brow raised. She nodded.

"We could bring the buggy, drive across. That is, if Rowan is in Chernobog's realm instead of Eris's."

"Let's hope she's in Eris's realm, then," Ana said. "Because Despotiko was just an empty island. Not difficult to access at all."

"If we've been briefed on all details and are prepared, you could consult your mirror now," Jude said.

I couldn't help but appreciate how good a teacher she was. Yes, we were in the middle of the most important fight of my life. Saving my sister was everything, and success was paramount.

But I was also still in training here at the Academy. This had become part of it, an advanced fast lane brought on by circumstance. And Jude helped guide me, but never took control.

I smiled at her and nodded, then looked around the table, waiting for anyone to pipe up with more info. No one did.

"Guess we're ready to look." I drew in a ragged breath as Ana pulled the mirror from her bag.

She stood, and flicked off the lights. "I'm standing near the door. I'll hold out the mirror and ask to see Rowan. Everyone stay quiet. Look for details in the image to figure out where she is. We won't speak to her in case she's currently in one of her bad spells."

Everyone stayed dead silent, and Ana counted down to zero.

The mirror flared to life. It was roughly the size of a dinner plate, and glowed with orange light. I squinted.

There was flame. From a torch.

It illuminated Rowan, who sat in a large window seat, seeming high in a tower. My heart pounded against my ribs, and I prayed she couldn't hear. We didn't need her alerting the guards and going somewhere else.

I studied the area around her. There were heavy stone walls, black with grime. But they were shiny. Black ice? Outside of the window, snow fell, though the land beyond was bare. Wind whipped the white flakes through the air.

The image went dark.

There was silence.

Finally, Hedy spoke. "I think that's it. The connection is broken."

Ana flipped on the light and joined us.

"It was Chernobog's realm," Belobog said. "Ice and dark. Just like him."

"I have to agree," Cass said. "Highly unlikely that it's snowing in Eris's Greek realm."

Dang.

"She's in his castle," Belobog said. "It won't be hard to find, but entering will be difficult. Stealth is a must."

"Then we know where we are going." I stood. "I understand if this is too dangerous for volunteers—"

Ali laughed. Haris joined him.

I smiled at them. "All right, then. We'll meet at the buggy on the front lawn in fifteen minutes. I'm going to need to find Emily to see if she'll transport us all."

"Wear black," Cade said. "We'll try to blend in."

The group stood, and we scattered.

Cass joined me in the hall. "Would you like me to call Nix and Del to come help? They'll be here in a heartbeat."

Warmth filled my chest, and I shot her a grateful look before turning my gaze to Ana. "The buggy is at max capacity, isn't it?"

Ana nodded. "Between all of us, yes."

"But I can fit, right?" Cass said.

I nodded. "Thank you."

"Of course. And Belobog is right. Stealth is often everything."

Our team was strong enough to win this. As long as we could get inside the castle walls before they whisked Rowan away, we would save her.

Fifteen minutes later, after dressing entirely in black winter clothes and finding Emily to transport us, I met the group on the front lawn.

Ana had been in charge of picking up the buggy from the stables, and she sat behind the wheel with Caro and Ali next to her. Haris, Cass, and Cade sat in the back. Belobog stood on the front platform, glowing golden and looking quite pleased with his position up front. While Cass could transport a lot of people, only Emily was strong enough to transport a whole car.

Emily and I joined them, climbing onto the back platform. Jude stood off to the side, along with Hedy.

Her stern gaze turned to me. "Be safe. If something goes wrong, use your comms charms for backup."

"Thank you." I wanted to hug her, but resisted, and turned toward Emily. "Ready whenever you are."

"I'll join Belobog. He can lead me there." Emily climbed over the back seats, seeming to intentionally step on Ali—no idea what was going on there—and joined Belobog on the front. She reached for his hand, and he seemed to know the drill, gripping hers quickly. She turned to us. "Hold on to your seats. This is going to be a bumpy ride."

I smiled and gripped the front railing, crouching low. The ether sucked us in, sending my stomach pitching, then spat us out into a dimly lit field. The weak sun tried to shine through the heavy black fog, but was doing a poor job of it.

Dark magic welled, turning my stomach sour.

"Ugh," Haris said. "Worse than I remember."

Belobog shuddered and climbed off the buggy. "This is where I must leave you. I can go no farther toward his realm, or his darkness would snuff out my light." He pointed directly ahead. "Go northwest. By the pinnacle of rock, there is a hole in the sea. That will take you to Chernobog's realm."

"Will it take us back out again?" Haris asked.

Good question.

"It will. Be safe on your journey. If you can kill Chernobog, you will clear this land and the people may return. The local covens are holding the dark magic back from spreading, but they are losing strength."

"Good motivation," Cade murmured.

That it was.

Emily climbed down and turned to us. "I'll hang with Belobog. When you need a lift back, call me. I'll be ready."

"Thanks, Emily." She wasn't a fighter, so I appreciated her coming this far into danger.

"Anytime. You're one of us."

People kept saying that. And it was corny, but I didn't care. In fact, I freaking loved it.

Ana revved the engine, and took off, leaving them behind. I waved, then turned to put my face into the wind.

The field quickly gave way to a forest where the trees were

gnarled and bent. They weren't dead, though, just covered with a strange, inky dust.

"This is why the world needs balance." Cass shuddered hard.

The buggy bounced over roots and wove around trees, making quick time through the dark forest. But the ugly energy of the place made me shiver. The closer we got to the coast, the stronger it felt.

Chernobog's influence was out of control.

A small flash of light caught my eye, and I turned. Squinted.

A pair of flashing eyes watched us. Two pairs. Three.

"Guys..." I said.

"We see it." Cass rose, standing on the seat, her gaze alert.

Caro joined her. Ali and Haris stayed seated, wisely. They needed to be closer to their prey, and standing would just put them in the way of the girls' firepower. Cade joined me on the back platform and drew his sword.

I powered up my lightning, ready to strike from the sky.

When the first monster leapt out at us, surprise flared in my chest. Panic flared as my eyes landed on the scaly black beast that flew from the tree limbs above. Long fangs and claws shined white, dripping with a green venom that made my skin itch to look at it.

Caro flung her hand out, shooting a piercing spray of water at the beast. It plunged through the creature's chest, and the monster exploded in a poof of black dust.

"They're magic," Cade said.

Cass nodded. "Probably the concentrated essence of Chernobog's evil."

Another flew from the right. Cass threw a fireball that lit up the night sky, and the monster exploded into dust.

Then they all came at once, flying from the trees like little bombs. Caro shot water, and Cass threw flame. I drew my sword, wanting to preserve my magic, charged for the beast that was nearly upon us, and stabbed it in the stomach.

The creature exploded into a poof of dust, the dark magic reeking. Cade followed suit, so fast with his sword that he made confetti of the beasts.

But they kept coming, faster and faster, until there was no way for us to fight them all. They landed on the car and lunged with their claws outstretched.

I kicked one away, but another sliced through my thigh with its razor-sharp claws. The poison burned.

"Take the wheel!" Ana cried.

Ali leaned over and grabbed the wheel, while Ana scrambled onto the front platform. She flung out her hands, and her glowing white shield burst forth.

The monsters bounced off like footballs, while the rest of us cleared the decks of the ones that had made it through the shield.

I was panting by the time they were gone, my wound burning like the devil.

"Are you all right?" Cade asked.

I winced and bent down, inspecting it. "Yeah. It's shallow."

"But the poison."

"Stings, but it's going away." I called on my healing power, forcing the poison from my body. The green goo dripped from the wound, followed by fresh blood, then the gash knit back together.

"Your magic is seriously badass," Caro said.

"Thanks." And damned if I wasn't grateful now. I'd never felt the need for super magic—I'd gotten by just fine in Death Valley using my sonic boom power—but when it came time to save someone I loved, I was damned glad to be a fighting and healing machine.

And since this skill could translate into a really satisfying career and the Protectorate, I had two reasons to appreciate it.

"Trade me back," Ana said once we'd driven out of the monster's territory.

She and Ali switched places, and she took the wheel, driving us out of the forest. Far in the distance, the ocean gleamed black. There was a long stretch of flat land to cross before we reached it. A small village sat in the middle, totally abandoned.

Ana drove slowly past, and we all peered at the buildings, searching for any signs of life.

There were none. It was quaint and very medieval-German looking, with thatched cottages and wood trim. Roses were dead on the vines and bushes withered. A beer stein sat abandoned on an outdoor table.

"It looks like Octoberfest caught an evil curse," Cass said.

"No kidding." Sadness welled in my chest. "But it was a nice place once."

Cade gripped my shoulder, his touch comforting. "We'll stop that bastard Chernobog. His power and magic once had a place in the world, but if this is what he chooses to do with it—to *abuse* it—he must be stopped."

I reached up and touched his hand. "Thanks."

As we drove, I scanned the terrain in front of us, my gaze finally catching on a pillar of stone that rose up from the sea. I pointed. "There!"

Ana turned the buggy toward the stone, and we bounced toward the sea. I leapt off as soon as she parked, hurrying toward the water.

The shore was a small stone cliff that fell five feet into the roiling black ocean. Right beneath the pillar, there was a hole in the water.

"Whoa," Ana breathed.

"Creepy," Caro added.

I had to agree. The hole was ten feet across, with water pouring down on all sides. I couldn't see down, even with Heimdall's vision.

I looked up at everyone. "I don't mind if you stay here."

"As if." Ali grinned, then jumped into the hole.

My stomach pitched as I watched him disappear into the darkness. But there was no time to dawdle. I pressed a quick kiss to Cade's cheek and leapt into the hole behind Ali.

The wind tore at my hair as I plummeted through the darkness, the water rushing by on both sides.

Five seconds later, I landed on the ground with a crash, somehow staying on my feet. Ali stood in the darkness of this new realm, a sickly smile on his face. He was trying to be cocky, but the magic here was so dark—so evil—that it was impossible to wear a normal smile.

I joined him, wrapping an arm around his shoulder and squeezing. "You're a good friend."

He hugged me. "Back at ya'."

We separated and turned to inspect our surroundings more closely, our friends flying out of the portal behind us.

The world was dark here, the pale moon illuminating the snow that whipped on the wind. Despite the white flakes that flecked through the air, the ground was barren black rock. Snowflakes drifted across it, but never settled. In the distance, a mountain rose up, topped by a shining black castle.

Ali whistled. "That's some fortress he's got."

"No kidding." Chernobog was darkness on steroids.

I turned to my friends. "I'll try to keep us invisible. We'll make our way to the castle as quickly as possible, find a way to break in, then Cass—could you lead us straight to Rowan? We have to get this antidote to her so we can get her away from them."

Cass saluted. "Aye aye."

"We won't be able to see each other like this, so if you get into trouble, shout. Otherwise, I'll try to keep up a running commentary so you can follow my voice."

"What will you talk about?" Ana asked.

"Not a clue."

"How about a story?" Haris asked. "Like a book on tape."

"I wish I were that clever." I called upon Loki's magic, shielding us with invisibility, then I took off at a jog. "Well, guys, I've got no idea what to talk about, so I'll sing us a song."

I sang a ditty that I remembered from my childhood about a baby beluga whale, using Heimdall's hearing to count the footfalls of my friends. Fortunately, I could hear everyone well, and it was easy to make sure my friends were with me. Unfortunately, "Baby Beluga" was only about thirty seconds long. So I launched into a repeat. And another repeat after that.

Someone chuckled—Cade, I thought—and I couldn't blame him. Singing a nursery rhyme as we tried to storm an evil god's castle was high on my list of the ridiculous.

We were halfway across the dark field, the castle looming ever higher, when the first shadowy figure flew toward us. It wore tattered robes and had no face—just blackness within the hood.

Fear chilled my skin as I drew my sword and lunged for the thing.

My steel sliced through the middle of the wraith, but the creature didn't stop. Just flew right into me, merging with my body.

I gasped as sickness filled me, a queasiness that nearly sent me to my knees. Chills followed, then fever.

"Sickness wraiths." Cade's voice was rough with pain.

I lost my grip on the invisibility, and everyone appeared around me. More wraiths flew at our group, racing around us.

Through us. They didn't stay with us long, but just their touch wracked us with illness. Queasiness, chills.

I shuddered.

Caro shot her deadly streams of water while Cass threw flames, but the wraiths were impenetrable. Even Ali and Haris couldn't possess them. My steel did nothing, nor did Cade's.

Ana tried her shield, but they blew right through it.

Our running stumbled to a stop, and we nearly went to our knees. Every one of us was white as a sheet, skin clammy.

We were failing, and we couldn't fight these wraiths.

12

Ana screwed up her face, rage seeming to overtake her. Her frustration radiated out in waves.

I felt it, too.

So close! We were so close to Rowan.

Yet so freaking far.

And none of my magic worked against these beasts. And no new powers were arriving.

Helplessness welled in me, tears pricking my eyes as my insides coiled.

Come on, Norse gods!

I needed them, and they were leaving me hanging.

Suddenly, light glowed from Ana, pale but fierce. I could barely see it, and no one else seemed to notice. My vision from Heimdall made it possible?

The light stretched out from her, hitting the wraiths. They hissed and shrank back. The light glowed, bringing with it a magic that repelled them.

The sickness faded from my muscles and bones. My stomach settled.

"What's happening?" Caro asked.

I stared at Ana, awed but unwilling to say anything. This was her deal. And some weird white magic was driving the wraiths away. No one else could see it, but it was definitely working.

Within moments, the wraiths were twenty yards off, rushing away. Ana's light was dim enough that I could barely see it—but it was there. And the energy felt good. Calm and pure.

"Let's go," Ana said, her expression shaken.

I couldn't blame her. New magic could be scary.

Strong once again, we took off at a run. We were in too much of a hurry for anyone to wonder out loud about our good luck. I called upon Loki's power, turning us invisible again, and resumed my impromptu performance of "Baby Beluga."

After a while, Ana's light faded, but we'd left the wraiths behind already. We'd need to figure out what the heck that was.

"Big mountain," Cass gasped out.

"No kidding," Caro said.

The mountain loomed tall and dark as we neared, an imposing structure that rose thousands of feet in the air. It stank of sulfur and death, and cold air wafted down from above. I shivered and huddled into my jacket as we began to climb. Jagged black rock and chips of ice shifted underfoot, so scrambling up was difficult. Every dozen yards or so, I'd skid on a large patch of ice and lose my footing.

As I slammed into the ground for the third time, Ana went down next to me. Pain flared in my knees, and the cold bit into my hands. She couldn't be doing any better, but we both rose silently and kept going.

I'd take all the bruises in the world if it meant saving Rowan.

Behind us, my friends were silent. Only Cade managed to stay on his feet the whole time, though Cass came in second for keeping her footing. All her time raiding ancient tombs for treasure had trained her well.

By the time we neared the base of the castle, the cold had

sunk into my bones. The black icy walls shot straight up into the air, three hundred feet tall if they were an inch.

I reached out to touch the side of the castle. Slick black ice froze my fingertips. The wall gleamed darkly, and I squinted at it.

Cass joined me, using her fire magic to create a ball of flame in the palm of her hand. It reflected in the slick ice of the wall, shining partially through to reveal ice that was many feet thick.

I squinted, but I couldn't see the other side. "Solid ice."

"Impossible to climb," Cade said. "Even with ice picks, it's still too slick. And guards would eventually see us. It'd take ages to get over."

I frowned. Too bad I wasn't strong enough to fly anyone over. Cass could only shift into a winged beast if she was around a mage who had that talent. Her Mirror Mage powers were limited in that way.

"I can burn through the wall," Cass said. "Just melt the ice away."

"Wouldn't that take ages?" Caro asked.

Cass grinned. "Not the way I do it."

I glanced at Ana and Cade, who both nodded. This was our best bet. Right now, no one was looking over the castle wall. But eventually, a guard might show. If Cass could get us into the ice wall, we'd be hidden while she completed the tunnel.

"Let's do it," I said. "Thank you."

Cass nodded and rubbed her hands together. "Step back, guys. Might be a bit touchy at first."

I did as she asked, slipping on the ice underfoot. Cade grabbed my arm before I could bite the dust. Or the ice. "Thanks."

Cass held out her hands, and flame burst forth, plowing into the side of the castle. It was silent, but brilliantly bright.

I swallowed hard, praying that no guards were looking over the edge. Fates, I hoped Rowan was in here.

Fortunately, the force of her flame dug about six feet into the ice wall in minutes. She entered the tunnel, and we followed. The guards might see the glow, but the ice was so thick and black, and the night so deep and dark, that hopefully they wouldn't notice.

"Just a little while longer," Cass muttered.

Her flame was cutting quickly through the wall, but it was a *thick* wall. Particularly at the base.

Melted water began to flow around our boots, and I directed it toward the side walls using Njord's power, keeping our feet dry. In temps like this, we'd get frostbite if we had wet feet.

The tunnel began to warm from the flame, and the ice water above dripped coldly onto our head.

When the flame finally burst through to the other side of the castle, we rushed out, damp and chilly.

I could see nothing within the dark space, but it felt cavernous. Something about the air and the slight echo, perhaps. It was the size of a football arena, or even larger.

"I can't see anything," Ana whispered.

"I'm trying to use my flame," Cass said. "But it's shedding no light."

I could feel the warmth of it though. "You're making flame right now, right?"

"I am. So no one step in front of me." The warmth died. "Actually, I should just kill it. Duh."

"Something about this place is absorbing all light," Cade murmured.

"Yep, my cell phone isn't glowing at all," Caro said.

"Neither is my lightstone ring," Cass said.

I blinked, squinting into the dark as tension plucked at my nerve endings. A shiver ran down my spine.

"Chernobog is the god of darkness," I said. "He's damn good at it."

"But what does the darkness hide?" Anxiety echoed in Ana's voice.

"That's what I'm afraid of." I stepped forward, moving my feet gingerly.

"Watch for cliffs," Caro said. "Shuffle your feet so you feel what's coming."

"I'll be careful." Something grabbed my foot, and I nearly shrieked.

Next to me, Ana hissed. "Something has my foot."

Shit.

Acid pounded through my veins as the grip on my foot tightened.

"It's got me, too." Caro's voice shook.

I jerked my foot away from the grip. It broke, a brittle snapping sound echoing in the darkness. I squinted, trying to see into nothing.

A crash sounded behind me, then a yelp.

"Help!" Caro whispered frantically, her voice rife with fear. "It's got me on my knees. Dragging me down. So tight."

I could hear so well I could almost imagine what was happening.

A grunting noise sounded. More brittle snapping.

"I got her," Ali said.

"My leg!" Caro said. More breaking noises. Caro had kicked, like I had. "They'll squeeze you to death!"

"Shit!" Cass's voice sounded.

A thump.

She'd been dragged to the floor.

I squinted around frantically, trying to see to help. Something shattered, and Cade grunted. "I got her."

"They're bones," Ana hissed. "I feel them."

"And they're trying to drag us down," Cass said. "Devour us."

"We have to run," Caro said. "Can't get caught by them."

"But drop-offs—"

A fierce grip clutched my calf and pulled me down, strong hands pulling at my thighs. They gripped me so hard that pain flared, biting into muscle and bone. I went to my knees on the ground, catching myself with my hands.

My palm closed over a skeletal hand just as another one reached up to grab my face.

I hissed in terror, trying to jerk away. But they were so strong!

It dragged me to the ground till I lay flat on my stomach, the arms wrapping around me, trying to crush me into the floor. I couldn't feel any bones beneath me, just the skeletal arms that reached out of the floor and clutched me to them, trying to crush me into the flagstone below.

Panic flared as the grip tightened unbearably. My bones threatened to snap.

I pushed and thrashed, trying to break free, a cry wringing from my throat. But at this angle and this grip, I couldn't move.

Strong, warm hands grabbed my waist and yanked me up, snapping the bones that bound me.

"I gotcha," Cade said.

"Thanks!"

Behind me, Cade fell to his knees, nearly pulling me down with him. The skeletal arms had grabbed him! He released me, and I turned, tugging at his arms to help him break the magical grasp of the skeletons.

"Go!" he rasped.

"I'm not leaving you." But it was damned hard to break their grasp.

Someone joined me—Ali or Haris, I thought—and yanked hard. We jerked Cade up. As soon as the first skeleton lost its grip, Cade surged away from the others, breaking their grip.

"We need to run," Ana said. "If they get us all on the ground, there's no one left to break us free."

"They'll crush our bones," Caro said.

She was right. "Fine! But shuffle. Don't go over the edge of a crevasse." There had been a crevasse deep in Gravensteen castle, and there could be one here.

We began to shuffle across the floor, kicking at the skeletal hands while searching for a drop-off in the floor. I called upon my wings, but didn't fly. I couldn't, not when I was at the front of the group. No way I'd take to safety when I could be the one scouting for a crevasse that might swallow us up.

If I'd designed this castle to repel people, that was what I would have done—built a whole bunch of creepy pits and scare people into them.

If I fell, I could at least fly upward.

The knowledge didn't keep a wild thundering from beating inside my chest, my heart going wild.

I squinted into the dark, claustrophobia crushing me. I knew this space was huge, but the dark made it tiny. The grabbing hands made it worse.

A tiny light shined from high above. I blinked, trying to see better. "Anyone see the light overhead?"

"Nothing," Cass said.

"Nada," Ana added.

I squinted at it. The thing flickered lightly. Too dim, but fighting. I could *feel* it.

Our shuffling was working so far, but we needed light to get out of this alive. I hated to leave them, particularly after thinking how important it was to scout the way, but that light could be our ticket out of here.

I needed to investigate. It'd only take a second. "Guys, I'm going to fly up to the light. Maybe I can get it to shine brighter. Watch your feet. Just fight them off. Don't go far."

"Be careful," Cade said.

I stretched my wings. "You be careful. Watch the damned ground and don't go far. I'll be back in a sec."

"Will do," Ana said.

I took off into the air, flying high. As soon as I left, a low shout sounded from below. Then a grunt.

"We need to go faster!" Ana said.

Shit.

They couldn't wait for me.

But they were right.

Of course it would get worse the farther we went into the pitch-black castle. I flew faster, the light overhead calling to me. I prayed there were no ledges or walls for me to smack into as I flew.

Below, I could hear my friends running. Fear shot through me. It was only a matter of time before the running became a really bad idea.

When I neared the light, I realized that it was a dingy crystal. A faint glow from within pulsed, trying to break free.

I drew my sword from the ether and stabbed upward toward the crystal.

My steel shattered the glass, and light burst forth. It blew me backward, and I tumbled wings over butt, blinded.

A sharp scream sounded from below. My stomach dropped as I righted myself and searched the ground.

The sight nearly made my wings stop moving.

A million skeletal arms reached out of the flagstone floor, waving as they tried to blindly catch whoever stepped over them. Cade and Ali were trying to drag Caro off the ground, but it was Ana who caught my eye.

She was clinging to the edge of a large pit. More gaping black holes dotted the space. There were *so many*.

I stored my sword in the ether and dove for Ana, wings

carrying me quickly through the air. Cass was racing for her, too, stumbling every few feet as a skeletal arm grabbed her legs. She blasted them away with her flame, a brilliant jet of orange death that I was grateful she hadn't used in the enchanted dark.

One of us would have eaten it, for sure.

Ana's terrified eyes met mine as a skeletal hand grabbed onto hers where it clutched the edge of the rock. It began to peel her fingers off.

I flew harder, lungs burning.

Just as I reached her, the white bones broke her grip on the rock, and she began to plummet.

I reached out, straining, praying.

I grabbed her wrist. Her hand wrapped around my own, her frantic gaze meeting mine.

I heaved, panting, as I tried to fly her out of the hole. My wings could barely support us both, and progress was slow. I was so close to the top edge of the pit, but couldn't make it over.

When a hand gripped my ankle, I instinctively kicked.

"Hey!" Cade said.

Oh, thank fates.

I stilled, and he hauled us up, aiding my wings. The skeletal hands clutched at us as we were dragged up onto solid ground, but I struck out, knocking them away.

The light made it easier to see and attack, and we scrambled upright.

"Run!" I sprinted across the floor, headed for an exit at the far side of the enormous cavern. It was another smaller cave, a dark semicircle that led to who knew where.

Didn't matter though. Had to be better than the skeleton graveyard riddled with pits of despair.

There were so many pits in the ground that I was grateful I'd found the light, even if it had been a risky move.

Caro shot fierce jets of water as she ran, clearing the way for us. It blasted the skeletal arms apart, and we sprinted forward.

By the time we ran under the dark archway, I was panting.

The room on the other side was much smaller. There were no immediate threats, so I turned around and peeked back at the cavernous room, unable to help myself.

The ground now lay still, no arms in sight. Probably triggered by intruders, or weight on the floor.

But it was the sight of the cells that circled the space that made me shudder. Ancient metal bars concealed small boxes that had once held prisoners. They were all empty, but the idea of them made bile rise in my throat.

"People were being kept down here," I murmured. "Amongst all this darkness and evil."

"No longer," Cade said. "And we'll take out Chernobog. For good."

I nodded, determined. Just like Cocidius, Chernobog was an evil bastard. And this was the evidence. I turned back to the square room.

"Maybe this was the guard's room," Cass said.

"I buy that," Ana said.

"Now it's just haunted." Ali shuddered. "You feel it?"

"I do." Haris moved closer to his twin. "This place has been abandoned a long time. Whatever horrible things happened here have turned it into a nightmare."

"The memory of true evil can create darkness," Caro said. "My gran used to tell me stories."

That must have been what happened back in the cell room. The evil had devoured the light, almost extinguishing it. I'd felt its energy. It was in this room, too.

As I stepped into the middle, the air grew hazy and gray in front of me.

"What the hell is that?" Ana murmured.

It coalesced into a line of figures, each wearing a black cloak and cowl.

"Twenty bucks they have no faces," Cass said.

Ana chuckled.

"Grim Reapers." Cade stepped forward just as they did.

Their dark magic rolled over me, making my heart stutter and slow. My mind followed, blurring at the edges. I nearly stumbled to my knees, gasping. I wanted to run, to scream, to escape.

But I couldn't. I was trapped.

Cold and weakness stole over me. Stealing my life force.

Ana gripped my hand, but her touch was icy and frail. "They're killing us."

The words were so soft, I could barely hear them. But she was right.

They were nothing like Death's minion, who we'd met back at Gravensteen. These were Grim Reapers, here to take their reward.

In front of us, black and silver light shimmered around Cade. His aura. The swell of his magic followed, the sound of clashing swords and the scent of a storm at sea. He shifted into his wolf form and growled.

The Grim Reapers shrank back.

He prowled forward, his lips pulled back from his fangs as a low rumble filled the room. The Grim Reapers continued to back up, drifting away from the wolf.

How had Cade known what to do?

This looked like a familiar dance—like death knew to fear the wolf.

Cade stalked forward, growling, pushing the Reapers back.

He was clearing a path for us!

And as the Reapers backed off, the dark tug of their magic

faded. It still slowed my heart and my mind—my body gradually fading—but I could move.

I staggered after Cade, my friends doing the same. Every step was a monumental effort, tearing through me like I was running the last mile of a marathon.

Cade's steps began to slow—this must be affecting him, too —but he kept going, lurching along.

Finally, he broke through the line of Reapers, and we struggled past them, picking up speed as we gained distance.

Sweat poured down my eyes as I lurched into a darkened stairwell, my friends at my side. Cade had shifted back to his human form and walked behind us, growling to hold off the Reapers.

"Go," Ana ordered.

I began to struggle up the stairs, strength gaining with every step.

"That was the flipping worst," Caro said.

We quickened our pace as our strength increased, and I glanced back. Cade followed behind, now in his human form.

When we reached a dark landing that was actually a fairly large room, I turned to him. "What was that?"

"The Grim Reaper is afraid of wolves. I'm the most dangerous wolf there is."

"Thank fates for that." I studied the room briefly. We were higher up in the castle. It was large and high-ceilinged, and I realized that much of the enormous height of the castle was because it was built on these great spaces below. This room was particularly uninteresting.

Except for a faint tug of recognition. *Rowan.* "You feel that?"

"I do." Ana approached the next flight of stairs, stepping onto the first. "She's here. Above."

The words had barely left her mouth when the floor in the

middle of the room exploded in an eruption of stones. They flew into the air, followed by a poof of dust.

I dived to the side, trying to avoid the massive rocks. Someone cried out in pain as I scrambled to my feet and spun around.

A giant stood in the middle of the room, having burst to the surface from down below. He was forty feet tall, with three heads. The middle head roared.

"Ah, shit. They're going to hear that," Ana said.

Yeah, our cover was officially blown.

When the giant breathed fire from his left head, nearly taking off my hair, I lunged to the side. Heat blazed, but flame didn't hit me. I rolled, hopping up in time to see his right head breathe an icy blast of breath that nearly hit Cade.

Fortunately, he was fast enough. But the breath coated a large stone block with so much ice that it doubled in size.

"Shit!" Ali cried. "The Belachko!"

"What's that?" I shot into the air, my wings carrying me high. I had to distract this guy from my friends.

"Some kind of Slavic monster," Haris said. "We read about him when hunting Chernobog."

"Duh, it's a monster!" Caro shouted.

"How do we kill it?" Cade demanded.

"When it runs out of fuel, it's easy to kill," Ali said. "I think that means its fiery and icy breath."

So we just had to distract it.

I darted around its heads, drawing my sword from the ether. The reek of his dark magic made me gag, visions of his evil deeds flashing in my mind.

Ugh, gross. His magical signature was some kind of weird mind thing where I could see exactly what he wanted to do to me. What he'd done to the prisoners who'd once lived here.

It was right out of my worst nightmares. Most of it, I never could have even thought up myself. Panic made my heart race.

We had to take him out. He couldn't be allowed to exist. Not something this evil.

From up here, I could definitely land a solid blow, taking out one of the heads.

His left head spun around, doing a full 180 until the monster glared at me with gleaming dark eyes. It opened its mouth, the scent of sulfur rolling over me, and emitted a blast of flame.

I was already dodging out of the way, but I was too slow. The flame touched my skin, heat searing, right before a blast of water from below doused it. I tumbled backward, my front aching.

Below, Caro shot her ferocious jet of water at the monster's flame, dousing it. I looked down to see a charred shirt and reddened flesh, but nothing was melted, thank fates.

Down below, Cass shot her flame at the monster's blasts of ice, protecting the others, who launched an attack at the giant's legs. Cass's left calf was bloody and torn—she must have been the one who had cried out. Had a flying stone gotten her?

Ana used her shield to protect Cass as she worked, while Caro darted around, trying to keep up with the monster's fire-breathing head.

Ali and Haris swung their swords so fast that I could barely see them, but they glanced off the giant's legs, not making contact. Cade tried to plunge his blade into the giant's shin, but it, too, bounced off.

The deadly blasts of ice and fire were starting to weaken, but we needed to get this guy off his feet if we wanted to deliver the kill shot when he ran out of fuel.

"Cade!" I said. "Let's hit him in the chest."

He nodded, shifting into his wolf form and backing up. I flew until I hovered over him, then counted to three.

On three, we charged. Cade leapt into the air, his form

graceful and strong. I hurled toward the giant's chest, and we hit him at the same time, the force of our blow sending him off his feet.

He crashed to the ground, and my friends leapt on him. His magical signature flared once again, gruesome images of torn apart people flashing in my mind.

Inhuman.

His fire and ice were nearly gone, and I flew down, plunging my blade into his chest. Ali and Haris approached from the sides, slicing their blades over his outer necks, while Caro decapitated his last head with a powerful stream of water.

I yanked my sword free as my friends stumbled away. I flew down to join them, then landed and closed my wings into my body.

"That was the worst." Cass shuddered.

"I've never seen anything like that." Cade rubbed his head, as if to banish the dark memories that the Belachko had forced into our minds.

If Cade, who'd seen dozens of wars, had never seen anything like that, then we knew this guy was *really* bad.

"Let's count that as our good deed," Ali said. "And get the hell out of here."

"One sister, coming up," Haris said.

I sure hoped they were right. Ana sprinted for the stairs, and I followed, but as I jumped on the stairwell, I caught sight of Cass, struggling to cross the room toward us.

"Hang on." I spun and knelt by her side, calling on my healing power and feeding it into her leg.

"Wow." Relief filled her voice. "You're good at that."

"Thanks." The skin on her leg knit together, and I stood.

It was only about thirty seconds, but by the time I finished, everyone else was out of the room.

"Let's go." I raced up the stairs, Cass behind me.

"They'll be up there," Cass said. "So be ready."

She was right. There was no way the Rebel Gods hadn't heard the commotion of the Belachko exploding out of the ground. That was probably his whole purpose. Stop the trespassers. Or, at least, make so much noise everyone else would freak out and start to fight, too.

Which meant I had to hightail it for Rowan as fast as I could.

When I spilled out onto a courtyard, icy wind whipped at my hair. The battle had already begun. Demons were leaping off the rampart walls, landing in the courtyard and drawing their swords. My friends were already fighting.

Ali and Haris used their Djinn powers to possess the demons, making them kill each other before leaping out of their bodies and slamming into some new ones.

Caro shot fierce jets of water, lancing through chests and delivering kill shots with deadly accuracy.

But it was the Rebel Gods who caught my eye. Two of them, leaping out of a massive window up above.

They were so determined to lay the smack down on us that they couldn't even use the freaking stairs.

Eris, her face dripping with blood, flew through the air like a terrible dream. Her white robes were streaked with crimson, and her blood-thirsty grin was narrowed in on Cass.

"Oh, this jerk is mine," Cass growled.

They'd fought before, back at the Rebel Gods' stronghold, and it looked like Eris wanted a repeat. Fortunately, so did Cass. She charged the Rebel God, her magic flaring.

It nearly sent me to my knees. I'd known Cass was megapowerful, but she was easily on the level of Cade. Without being a god. How did that work?

She shot her flame at Eris right before they collided, lighting the god's hair on fire. Eris shrieked, a sound of pure rage, and shoved Cass so hard she flew twenty feet through the air.

Fortunately, she landed with a roll, her catlike reflexes protecting her. With her ability as a Mirror Mage, she could give Eris a taste of her own medicine.

A roar from the side of the courtyard caught my ear, and I turned. Cade was charging Cocidius, and the two gods were about to collide in a clash of speed and violence.

Worry tore at my chest, but I shoved it away.

Cade was tough, and he was meant to fight the other Celtic war god. It just made sense. War god against war god.

I caught sight of Ana, who raced across the courtyard to the tall tower that sat in the middle.

Rowan had to be in there. I recalled the view from the window that she'd been sitting in. It had been high up, overlooking the land beyond. I glanced up, catching sight of a pale face in the window.

Then she was jerked back in.

Rowan!

But my wings wouldn't fit through that tiny window.

I sprinted, following Ana into the tower. She was about ten feet ahead of me.

She glanced over her shoulder and caught sight of me. "Hurry up!"

The spiral staircase ran along the edges of the wide tower, leaving an open space right in the middle. A *big* open space.

Jackpot.

I unfurled my wings and drew my sword, leaping into the air.

I flew past Ana, who was red with exertion. The air whipped at my hair, and I landed on a platform outside the door that I thought was Rowan's room.

Rage and desperation filled me with strength, and I kicked the door in, then strode inside, sword raised.

Chernobog was trying to grab Rowan, but she'd climbed

onto the top of a heavy bookshelf. She'd always been spry, but this was impressive.

Her gaze darted to mine, clear and blue. "Bree!"

The joy in her voice almost made my heart explode.

She recognized me!

I glanced up. The conical ceiling indicated that we were at the top of the tower. I called upon my lightning, determined to kill Chernobog while Rowan was still in a lucid state. I didn't need her helping him when I was trying to save her.

He was at least seven feet tall, and the snow that whipped around him foretold of dangerous powers. His power felt like ice rushing over my skin and sounded like the roar of a winter wind. It tasted of vomit and smelled like death. It nearly sent me to my knees.

The lightning crackled within me, strong and fierce. I called it from the heavens, urging Thor's power to come to me. The bolt cracked out of the sky, piercing through the conical roof, which blasted apart, tiles flying everywhere. The white bolt hit Chernobog where he stood.

He stumbled, going to his knees.

His roar tore through the room as he stumbled to his feet. He swung his head like a bull, eyes blazing when they caught sight of me.

"I'm here to take my sister back." *How, though?*

This guy was *strong*. He threw out his hand, a massive spear of black ice hurtling toward me. I lunged to the side, the ice grazing my waist and slicing deep. He powered up another, so fast I couldn't get to my feet.

Ana lunged into the room, casting her protective shield over me. The black ice spear shattered against it, but Ana went to her knees, her shield dissipating.

That had *never* happened before.

Fear lanced me like acid through my veins.

It only got worse when Rowan leapt off the bookcase.

But the move didn't look threatening. At least, not toward Chernobog.

"Shit. She's enchanted again," I said.

She ran to Chernobog's side and grabbed his arm. He dug into his pocket, a move that made my stomach drop. He hurled a rock to the ground, and a gold cloud billowed up.

"No!" Ana lunged.

Chernobog dragged a willing—but cloudy-eyed—Rowan into the golden fog, stealing her away.

Fear like I'd never known chilled my heart. I leapt to my feet, sprinting after them.

"No!" Cade's roar followed me. He must have come up the stairs after us. "Don't!"

The one word held so much meaning.

Don't go in there, or you'll die.

Everyone knew that jumping through random heavenly transport portals was a death wish. No way Chernobog was going to a place that would be safe.

I didn't care.

I was going to save Rowan, no matter what.

I leapt into the golden cloud, Cade's words echoing in my ears. When I stumbled out on the other side, the air was vastly warmer.

Ana tripped out of the portal behind me, slamming into my back.

Of course she'd come. I didn't want her to risk herself, but she was like me.

She'd come for Rowan. And me. No matter what.

And there was no way either of us could defeat Chernobog alone.

A bright moon shined on this new realm, highlighting the white marble columns that surrounded us. The smell of the sea hit my nose, and the breeze pulled my hair back from my face.

Eris's realm. We were in Greece.

In the distance, Chernobog pulled Rowan along.

"There!" I sprinted after them.

Ana followed.

Figures marched out from behind the columns, warriors in Ancient Greek garb. Their stony faces met mine, and I realized that they were actually statues. Fabulously painted statues, and definitely not human.

Didn't mean they couldn't put the hurt on us, though.

I called on Thor's power, drawing the lightning down from the sky. I gave it everything I had, a complex magical demand that had twenty spears of lightning striking toward the earth. The thunder deafened me, nearly sending me to my knees.

The lightning was no better, blinding me quickly. When it faded, all of the soldiers lay on the ground, cracked into a million pieces.

"Nice." Ana raced ahead, and I followed, shaking my head to recover from the bright white light.

My lungs burned as we ran after them.

As much as I wanted to catch them, I liked that he ran from us. It meant he feared us. I was terrified we couldn't beat him— but if *he* feared *us*?

Yeah, that was good.

I called upon Loki's illusion power, commanding it to create a massive tiger. The beast prowled out from behind the columns ahead of Chernobog, then roared, sprinting for him.

Chernobog stopped dead in his tracks, then turned.

A vicious scowl crossed his face as he spotted us.

"Nowhere to go," I shouted. "I control the tiger."

He had no way to know it was an illusion. I made flames burst up on either side of us as the tiger prowled behind.

"What magic is this?" he roared.

"I am a Dragon God!" My voice reverberated over the land, so powerful it shocked even me. "I am *all power*."

It wasn't true, but the nature of my magic meant I sure had a ton of it.

From the brief faltering expression on his face, he seemed like he might've believed me. Right now, *lots* of power and *all* the power were pretty much the same.

I prowled closer, calling on the magic that I had inside me. If I was going to kill him, I needed to create the biggest lightning bolt in the history of time. But I didn't want him to be holding on to Rowan, or she'd get some of the shock.

The magic gathered inside me as he hurled a black ice bolt at me. I called my shield from the ether, but the ice was so big that it collided with me and sent me flying onto my back. Pain flared.

Ana crouched over me, casting her protective shield. "I don't know if this will work against him for long. Every hit is like a Mack truck."

I scrambled to my feet, aching everywhere. Chernobog had Rowan's arm gripped in his hand, and he was studying the flames that trapped us in a circle. If he tried to break through them, he'd realize they were just an illusion.

With every bit of strength I could muster, I called upon a lightning bolt. Fortunately, Rowan had stepped away from him. Her cooperation had convinced him, maybe.

Or maybe it was because he was holding out both hands, ready to shoot a massive and deadly ice bolt that required two hands. Considering that the one-handed attack had nearly killed me, I didn't want to know about the two-handed attack.

I didn't hesitate, sending the lightning down toward him. It cracked through the sky, the scent of ozone burning my nose, and sent him to his knees.

Pale and drawn, he shook his head. Clearly not dead.

Damn it.

Next to him, Rowan's eyes turned blue.

Hope flared in my chest.

Her gaze darted to the large dagger sheathed at his side, then back to me.

I mouthed, "Wait."

She nodded, tension clearly vibrating in her shoulders, but she got what I was trying to say.

"We can't kill him alone." I glanced at Ana, then nodded toward Rowan.

Beside me, she glowed with a pale white light. It was the same light as before, back in Chernobog's realm, but it was spreading fast. So fast. It reached Chernobog in seconds. He turned white, gasping.

"You're doing that!"

"Holy fates, I am."

I called upon my lightning, wanting to add to the attack.

It crackled inside me. I reached toward the sky, harvesting every bit of energy that I could, until finally, it nearly burst out from the inside. I commanded it to hit Chernobog. The bolt shot down from the sky, striking him on top of the head.

He crashed to the ground.

Rowan jumped, grabbing the blade at his waist and plunging it into his heart. His neck.

She went wild, hacking him apart as blood sprayed.

"Shit." I raced for her. She was losing it.

Ana sprinted alongside, breath heaving. We stumbled to a halt by a blood-covered Rowan. The god was nothing but mincemeat from the waist up. She'd hit him so many times in the neck that his head was severed.

She looked up at us, panting.

Then her blue eyes clouded over.

Shit.

Ana lunged for her, throwing her to the ground. She sat on her chest. "Get the knife!"

I grabbed it out of Rowan's hand, throwing it aside.

She thrashed like a wild thing, but Ana held her down, determination adding to her strength. "We're not going to lose you now!"

I fumbled in my pocket and dug out the vial of antidote. It took everything I had to get the top off without spilling it. If we didn't get this down her throat, we would lose her again.

I will not lose Rowan.

With the open vial clutched in my hand, I lunged for her, pinching open her cheeks and pouring the liquid down her throat. She coughed and sputtered, but I closed her mouth and pinched her nose until she swallowed.

Guilt streaked through me—this was not how I imagined our first moments together—but when her blue eyes popped open, recognition and joy flared in their depths.

Tears sprang to my own eyes. "Rowan!"

Ana and I collapsed on her, hugging her. Chernobog's blood stuck to me, clogging my nose, but beneath it, I could smell Rowan.

"Your magic smells normal!" It hadn't before—one of the reasons I hadn't recognized her earlier. But now, I could smell the fresh scent of clover and taste honey on my tongue.

She squeezed tight. "Oh fates, I can't believe you found me."

Ana cried next to us, deep sobs that didn't allow any words through. Tears poured from my own eyes now.

Finally, we were together again.

I jerked back, remembering where we were.

Next to us, Chernobog's body was disappearing into the ground, being absorbed by the earth. A godly realm claiming one of its own?

Whatever the case... "We have to get out of here."

Ana gasped and straightened. "Yeah. They could follow."

"How the hell *do* we get out?" I asked.

"There's a portal." Rowan scrambled to her feet. She was so coated with blood that she looked like Carrie after the prom, but she was the best thing I'd seen in years. "Come on."

She sprinted across the ground, and we followed. I kept my

senses alert, trying to identify oncoming threats. Depending on how my friends did back at Chernobog's castle, we might have two more Rebel Gods on our tail.

Fear and guilt streaked through me at the thought.

I'd left them. It'd been part of the plan—approved by everyone—but still, guilt reared its ugly head.

Don't worry. My friends were strong. Cade was a damned god, and Cass was ridiculously powerful. Not to mention Caro, Ali, and Haris.

I had to have faith.

"There!" Rowan pointed to a glowing blue portal.

"Where does it go?"

"No idea!"

"Shit, really?" I stumbled to a stop in front of the portal.

"I only remember some things," she said. "Depends on how foggy I was at the time something happened."

"I'm so sorry for everything that's happened to you."

She looked me dead in the eye. "Not your fault. Not the time."

I blinked. She was right. We needed to run for it. Rowan had always been the practical one.

Right now, I was so used to danger in my life—and so *not* used to her—that I wanted to focus on her instead of getting the hell out of here. I could happily sit down and have a chat, entirely forgetting about the Rebel Gods on our tail.

And that was really freaking dumb.

"Let's go, then," I said. "Because this is the most dangerous place we could be."

At that, energy popped in the air. I turned, drawn by the sensation. Far in the distance, two figures stood.

Eris and Cocidius. Their power rolled toward us.

I turned back. "Go!"

Rowan leapt through the portal, and we followed, stumbling

out onto a rocky cliff. The morning sun peeked over the horizon, illuminating the gleaming blue sea that surrounded the rock upon which we stood.

I turned, realizing that we were actually inside a large, ruined temple. The broken white columns speared toward the air.

"We're on Despotiko Island. The entrance to Eris's realm," Ana said. "I was here with Cass."

"And those gods are coming after us," I said. "Run."

We sprinted away from them, but I had no idea where we were going. There was nothing on this island. It was just a freaking *rock*.

"Should we jump into the sea?" Ana asked. "Maybe there's a sea cave we can hide in."

"I could use a bath," Rowan said.

I laughed, forgetting how funny she was. If we could jump into the sea and find a sea cave, that would be ideal to hide in. But... "There could be sharks. And Rowan, you smell like a shark cookie right now."

"Good point."

But we couldn't fight two gods. We'd barely managed to take out one. My heart thundered as the seconds ticked by. Fear chilled my skin. They were going to jump through that portal any minute now.

Fifty yards away, two figures appeared out of the blue.

Cass and Cade.

"Holy fates!" I sprinted toward them, Rowan and Ana racing to keep up.

"Who's that?" Rowan asked.

"Our ride out of here," Ana said. "We're going home."

I couldn't believe our luck.

EPILOGUE

Two days later, after Cass had used her transporter power to get us off Despotiko before the Rebel Gods caught us, I sat with Ana and Rowan at the back of the Whisky and Warlock. We were lined up on a bench against the wall. Mayhem floated by my head, a ham clutched in her mouth, and a pink cocktail called the Witch's Rebellion sat on the table in front of me. Ana and Rowan had the same.

"I can't believe this is our new life." Rowan gazed around, eyes wide.

"Like it?" I took in the heavy logs in the ceiling and the ancient walls. The fire flickered warmly, and the sound of bagpipes filtered in from out on the street.

"Yeah." She leaned against me, wrapping her arm around me. "I don't care where we are. As long as we're together."

I leaned against her, and Ana did the same. My gaze drifted over the crowd in the small room where the Protectorate usually hung out after work. Caro, Ali, and Haris were leaning on the bar, while Jude and Hedy had a little corner table. Even Cass, Nix, and Del had shown up, saying that they liked the vibe of this place.

I secretly thought they just wanted to check on us, which was confirmed when Cass's gaze roved over us and she smiled. I grinned back, nodding my thanks to her, then my gaze drifted on. It collided with Cade's, who stepped through the door, his dark hair windblown and his cheeks ruddy.

He was so handsome I sighed.

"That's really your boyfriend?" Rowan asked. "Because, *meeeeow*."

"Not my boyfriend." At least, we hadn't talked about it.

Ana scoffed. "Whatever. He is."

"Caro said he fought like a madman back at Chernobog's realm. Took out all those demons in minutes," Rowan said.

He had. Apparently my friends had fought Cocidius and Eris for a while, until the Rebel Gods had figured out that Chernobog had run for it with Rowan. At that point, they'd disappeared, too, coming after us. It'd been quick work for them to kill the rest of the demons, then race for the portal so they could come after us. If Cass hadn't had the ability to teleport and we hadn't found our way back to Earth, we'd be dead. Or captured by the Rebel Gods.

"So you're not disappointed that we're no longer in Death Valley?" I asked.

"Heck no. That life is done. This is better." Her gaze shifted around, her wariness obvious. "Safer."

"You don't look like you feel safe." My heart twisted.

Her lips pressed together, and she reached for my hand. "Don't worry about me. I'll get over it."

"Five years." It tortured me to think what she'd been through all that time, a captive.

On the other side of Rowan, Ana's eyes glinted with tears. "We tried to find you."

"I know. You never gave up."

"How do you know?" Ana's voice cracked.

"Because I wouldn't have given up."

I swallowed hard. I'd spent most of the last two days crying from joy or grief. Knowing what had happened to Rowan tore me apart.

"Don't worry." She squeezed my hand again, as if she could give me her strength. She'd always been the strong one. But oh, how I wished I could have taken her place. "Really. Because of the connection charm, I was enchanted out of my mind most of the time. It was a blessing."

"So you don't have terrible memories?" Ana asked.

She'd refused to talk about it until now. Maybe it was the Witch's Rebellion that loosened her tongue, but I was terrified of what I'd hear. I stiffened my spine. I *had* to hear it, though. If she'd had to live it, I had to know. So I could get the bastards who'd taken her.

"I do have memories," Rowan said. "But we're going to use them to destroy the Rebel Gods."

Dark satisfaction streaked through me.

"I mean it," Rowan said. "I can find them. I have enough memory that we can take them out. And we have to. Because they're after us."

"For our power," Ana said.

"Yes. They used mine to build the stronghold. But all along, their plan was to use me to kidnap you. They could only steal one of us five years ago, and it turned out to be me. And then I hunted you." Her gaze turned dark. "I could have killed you."

"You were under a deep enchantment. That black oil you were coated with made you...not yourself," Ana said.

"I wasn't myself." Rowan shook her head. "But still, the idea of what I could have done... They gave me different powers. I was a puppet."

"A puppet no longer. And we'll get them before they get us," I said.

I wanted it for vengeance. For safety.

Hell, it didn't matter why I wanted it.

It had to be done. The Rebel Gods were evil, and we had to stop them.

And together, we had a chance.

THANK YOU FOR READING!

I hope you enjoyed *Attack by Magic*. Reviews are *so* helpful to authors. If you want to leave one, you can do so on Amazon GoodReads.

Join my mailing list at www.linseyhall.com/subscribe to stay updated. You'll also get a free ebook copy of *Hidden Magic*. The story stars Cass, Del, and Nix, the FireSouls who help Bree in the final battle of this book.

EXCERPT OF HIDDEN MAGIC

Jungle, Southeast Asia
  Five years before the events in Ancient Magic

"How much are we being paid for this job again?" I glanced at the dudes filling the bar. It was a motley crowd of supernaturals, many of whom looked shifty as hell.

"Not nearly enough for one as dangerous as this." Del frowned at the man across the bar, who was giving her his best sexy face. There was a lot of eyebrow movement happening. "Is he having a seizure?"

"Looks like it." Nix grinned. "Though I gotta say, I wasn't expecting this. We're basically in a tree, for magic's sake. In the middle of the jungle! Where are all these dudes coming from?"

"According to my info, there's a mining operation near here. Though I'd say we're more *under* a tree than *in* a tree."

"I'm with Cass," Del said. "Under, not in."

"Fair enough," Nix said.

We were deep in Southeast Asia, in a bar that had long ago

been reclaimed by the jungle. A massive fig tree had grown over and around the ancient building, its huge roots strangling the stone walls. It was straight out of a fairy tale.

Monks had once lived here, but a few supernaturals of inde-terminate species had gotten ahold of it and turned it into a watering hole for the local supernaturals. We were meeting our contact here, but he was late.

"Hey, pretty lady." A smarmy voice sounded from my left. "What are you?"

I turned to face the guy who was giving me the up and down, his gaze roving from my tank top to my shorts. He wasn't Clarence, our local contact. And if he meant "what kind of supernatural are you?" I sure as hell wouldn't be answering. That could get me killed.

"Not interested is what I am," I said.

"Aww, that's no way to treat a guy." He grabbed my hip, rubbed his thumb up and down.

I smacked his hand away, tempted to throat-punch him. It was my favorite move, but I didn't want to start a fight before Clarence got here. Didn't want to piss off our boss.

The man raised his hands. "Hey, hey. No need to get feisty. You three sisters?"

I glanced at Nix and Del, at their dark hair that was so different from my red. We were all about twenty, but we looked nothing alike. And while we might call ourselves sisters—*deir-fiúr* in our native Irish—this idiot didn't know that.

"Go away." I had no patience for dirt bags who touched me without asking. "Run along and flirt with your hand, because that's all the action you'll be getting tonight."

His face turned a mottled red, and he raised a fist. His magic welled, the scent of rotten fruit overwhelming.

He thought he was going to smack me? Or use his magic against me?

Ha.

I lashed out, punching him in the throat. His eyes bulged and he gagged. I kneed him in the crotch, grinning when he keeled over.

"Hey!" A burly man with a beard lunged for us, his buddy beside him following. "That's no way—"

"To treat a guy?" I finished for him as I kicked out at him. My tall, heavy boots collided with his chest, sending him flying backward. I never used my magic—didn't want to go to jail and didn't want to blow things up—but I sure as hell could fight.

His friend raised his hand and sent a blast of wind at us. It threw me backward, sending me skidding across the floor.

By the time I'd scrambled to my feet, a brawl had broken out in the bar. Fists flew left and right, with a bit of magic thrown in. Nothing bad enough to ruin the bar, like jets of flame, because no one wanted to destroy the only watering hole for a hundred miles, but enough that it lit up the air with varying magical signatures.

Nix conjured a baseball bat and swung it at a burly guy who charged her, while Del teleported behind a horned demon and smashed a chair over his head. I'd always been jealous of Del's ability to sneak up on people like that.

All in all, it was turning into a good evening. A fight between supernaturals was fun.

"Enough!" the bartender bellowed. "Or no more beer!"

The patrons quieted immediately. Fights might be fun, but they weren't worth losing beer over.

I glared at the jerk who'd started it. There was no way I'd take the blame, even though I'd thrown the first punch. He should have known better.

The bartender gave me a look and I shrugged, hiking a thumb at the jerk who'd touched me. "He shoulda kept his hands to himself."

"Fair enough," the bartender said.

I nodded and turned to find Nix and Del. They'd grabbed our beers and were putting them on a table in the corner. I went to join them.

We were a team. Sisters by choice, ever since we'd woken in a field at fifteen with no memories other than those that said we were FireSouls on the run from someone who had hurt us. Who was hunting us.

Our biggest goal, even bigger than getting out from under our current boss's thumb, was to save enough money to buy concealment charms that would hide us from the monster who hunted us. He was just a shadowy memory, but it was enough to keep us running.

"Where is Clarence, anyway?" I pulled my damp tank top away from my sweaty skin. The jungle was damned hot. We couldn't break into the temple until Clarence gave us the information we needed to get past the guard at the front. And we didn't need to spend too much longer in this bar.

Del glanced at her watch, her blue eyes flashing with annoyance. "He's twenty minutes late. Old Man Bastard said he should be here at eight."

Old Man Bastard—OMB for short—was our boss. His name said it all. Del, Nix, and I were FireSouls, the most despised species of supernatural because we could steal other magical being's powers if we killed them. We'd never done that, of course, but OMB didn't care. He'd figured out our secret when we were too young to hide it effectively and had been blackmailing us to work for him ever since.

It'd been four years of finding and stealing treasure on his behalf. Treasure hunting was our other talent, a gift from the dragon with whom legend said we shared a soul. No one had seen a dragon in centuries, so I wasn't sure if the legend was even true, but dragons were covetous, so it made sense they had a knack for finding treasure.

"What are we after again?" Nix asked.

"A pair of obsidian daggers," Del said. "Nice ones."

"And how much is this job worth?" Nix repeated my earlier question. Money was always on our minds. It was our only chance at buying our freedom, but OMB didn't pay us enough for it to be feasible anytime soon. We kept meticulous track of our earnings and saved like misers anyway.

"A thousand each."

"Damn, that's pathetic." I slouched back in my chair and stared up at the ceiling, too bummed about our crappy pay to even be impressed by the stonework and vines above my head.

"Hey, pretty ladies." The oily voice made my skin crawl. We just couldn't get a break in here. I looked up to see Clarence, our contact.

Clarence was a tall man, slender as a vine, and had the slicked back hair and pencil-thin mustache of a 1940s movie star. Unfortunately, it didn't work on him. Probably because his stare was like a lizard's. He was more Gomez Addams than Clark Gable. I'd bet anything that he liked working for OMB.

"Hey, Clarence," I said. "Pull up a seat and tell us how to get into the temple."

Clarence slid into a chair, his movement eerily snakelike. I shivered and scooted my chair away, bumping into Del. The scent of her magic flared, a clean hit of fresh laundry, as she no doubt suppressed her instinct to transport away from Clarence. If I had her gift of teleportation, I'd have to repress it as well.

"How about a drink first?" Clarence said.

Del growled, but Nix interjected, her voice almost nice. She had the most self control out of the three of us. "No can do, Clarence. You know... Mr. Oribis"—her voice tripped on the name, probably because she wanted to call him OMB—"wants the daggers soon. Maybe next time, though."

"Next time." Clarence shook his head like he didn't believe her. He might be a snake, but he was a clever one. His chest puffed up a bit. "You know I'm the only one who knows how to get into the temple. How to get into any of the places in this jungle."

"And we're so grateful you're meeting with us. Mr. Oribis is so grateful." Nix dug into her pocket and pulled out the crumpled envelope that contained Clarence's pay. We'd counted it and found—unsurprisingly—that it was more than ours combined, even though all he had to do was chat with us for two minutes. I'd wanted to scream when I'd seen it.

Clarence's gaze snapped to the money. "All right, all right."

Apparently his need to be flattered went out the window when cash was in front of his face. Couldn't blame him, though. I was the same way.

"So, what are we up against?" I asked.

The temple containing the daggers had been built by supernaturals over a thousand years ago. Like other temples of its kind, it was magically protected. Clarence's intel would save us a ton of time and damage to the temple if we could get around the enchantments rather than breaking through them.

"Dvarapala. A big one."

"A gatekeeper?" I'd seen one of the giant, stone monster statues at another temple before.

"Yep." He nodded slowly. "Impossible to get through. The temple's as big as the Titanic—hidden from humans, of course —but no one's been inside in centuries, they say."

Hidden from humans was a given. They had no idea supernaturals existed, and we wanted to keep it that way.

"So how'd you figure out the way in?" Del asked. "And why

haven't you gone in? Bet there's lots of stuff you could fence in there. Temples are usually full of treasure."

"A bit of pertinent research told me how to get in. And I'd rather sell the entrance information and save my hide. It won't be easy to get past the booby traps in there."

Hide? Snakeskin, more like. Though he had a point. I didn't think he'd last long trying to get through a temple on his own.

"So? Spill it," I said, anxious to get going.

He leaned in, and the overpowering scent of cologne and sweat hit me. I grimaced, held my breath, then leaned forward to hear his whispers.

As soon as Clarence walked away, the communications charms around my neck vibrated. I jumped, then groaned. Only one person had access to this charm.

I shoved the small package Clarence had given me into my short's pocket and pressed my fingertips to the comms charm, igniting its magic.

"Hello, Mr. Oribis." I swallowed my bile at having to be polite.

"Girls," he grumbled.

Nix made a gagging face. We hated when he called us girls.

"Change of plans. You need to go to the temple tonight."

"What? But it's dark. We're going tomorrow." He never changed the plans on us. This was weird.

"I need the daggers sooner. Go tonight."

My mind raced. "The jungle is more dangerous in the dark. We'll do it if you pay us more."

"Twice the usual," Del said.

A tinny laugh echoed from the charm. "Pay *you* more? You're lucky I pay you at all."

I gritted my teeth and said, "But we've been working for you for four years without a raise."

"And you'll be working for me for four more years. And four after that. And four after that." Annoyance lurked in his tone. So did his low opinion of us.

Del's and Nix's brows crinkled in distress. We'd always suspected that OMB wasn't planning to let us buy our freedom, but he'd dangled that carrot in front of us. What he'd just said made that seem like a big fat lie, though. One we could add to the many others he'd told us.

An urge to rebel, to stand up to the bully who controlled our lives, seethed in my chest.

"No," I said. "You treat us like crap, and I'm sick of it. Pay us fairly."

"I treat you like *crap,* as you so eloquently put it, because that is exactly what you are. *FireSouls.*" He spit the last word, imbuing it with so much venom I thought it might poison me.

I flinched, frantically glancing around to see if anyone in the bar had heard what he'd called us. Fortunately, they were all distracted. That didn't stop my heart from thundering in my ears as rage replaced the fear. I opened my mouth to shout at him, but snapped it shut. I was too afraid of pissing him off.

"Get it by dawn," he barked. "Or I'm turning one of you in to the Order of the Magica. Prison will be the least of your worries. They might just execute you."

I gasped. "You wouldn't." Our government hunted and imprisoned—or destroyed—FireSouls.

"Oh, I would. And I'd enjoy it. The three of you have been more trouble than you're worth. You're getting cocky, thinking you have a say in things like this. Get the daggers by dawn, or one of you ends up in the hands of the Order."

My skin chilled, and the floor felt like it had dropped out from under me. He was serious.

"Fine." I bit off the end of the word, barely keeping my voice from shaking. "We'll do it tonight. Del will transport them to you as soon as we have them."

"Excellent." Satisfaction rang in his tone, and my skin crawled. "Don't disappoint me, or you know what will happen."

The magic in the charm died. He'd broken the connection.

I collapsed back against the chair. In times like these, I wished I had it in me to kill. Sure, I offed demons when they came at me on our jobs, but that was easy because they didn't actually die. Killing their earthly bodies just sent them back to their hell.

But I couldn't kill another supernatural. Not even OMB. It might get us out of this lifetime of servitude, but I didn't have it in me. And what if I failed? I was too afraid of his rage—and the consequences—if I didn't succeed.

"Shit, shit, shit." Nix's green eyes were stark in her pale face. "He means it."

"Yeah." Del's voice shook. "We need to get those daggers."

"Now," I said.

"I wish I could just conjure a forgery," Nix said. "I really don't want to go out into the jungle tonight. Getting past the Dvarapala in the dark will suck."

Nix was a conjurer, able to create almost anything using just her magic. Massive or complex things, like airplanes or guns, were outside of her ability, but a couple of daggers wouldn't be hard.

Trouble was, they were a magical artifact, enchanted with the ability to return to whoever had thrown them. Like boomerangs. Though Nix could conjure the daggers, we couldn't enchant them.

"We need to go. We only have six hours until dawn." I grabbed my short swords from the table and stood, shoving them into the holsters strapped to my back.

A hush descended over the crowded bar.

I stiffened, but the sound of the staticky TV in the corner made me relax. They weren't interested in me. Just the news, which was probably being routed through a dozen techno-witches to get this far into the jungle.

The grave voice of the female reporter echoed through the quiet bar. "The FireSoul was apprehended outside of his apartment in Magic's Bend, Oregon. He is currently in the custody of the Order of the Magica, and his trial is scheduled for tomorrow morning. My sources report that execution is possible."

I stifled a crazed laugh. Perfect timing. Just what we needed to hear after OMB's threat. A reminder of what would happen if he turned us into the Order of the Magica. The hush that had descended over the previously rowdy crowd—the kind of hush you get at the scene of a big accident—indicated what an interesting freaking topic this was. FireSouls were the bogeymen. *I* was the bogeyman, even though I didn't use my powers. But as long as no one found out, we were safe.

My gaze darted to Del and Nix. They nodded toward the door. It was definitely time to go.

As the newscaster turned her report toward something more boring and the crowd got rowdy again, we threaded our way between the tiny tables and chairs.

I shoved the heavy wooden door open and sucked in a breath of sticky jungle air, relieved to be out of the bar. Night creatures screeched, and moonlight filtered through the trees above. The jungle would be a nice place if it weren't full of things that wanted to kill us.

"We're never escaping him, are we?" Nix said softly.

"We will." Somehow. Someday. "Let's just deal with this for now."

We found our motorcycles, which were parked in the lot

with a dozen other identical ones. They were hulking beasts with massive, all-terrain tires meant for the jungle floor. We'd done a lot of work in Southeast Asia this year, and these were our favored forms of transportation in this part of the world.

Del could transport us, but it was better if she saved her power. It wasn't infinite, though it did regenerate. But we'd learned a long time ago to save Del's power for our escape. Nothing worse than being trapped in a temple with pissed off guardians and a few tripped booby traps.

We'd scouted out the location of the temple earlier that day, so we knew where to go.

I swung my leg over Secretariat—I liked to name my vehicles —and kicked the clutch. The engine roared to life. Nix and Del followed, and we peeled out of the lot, leaving the dingy yellow light of the bar behind.

Our headlights illuminated the dirt road as we sped through the night. Huge fig trees dotted the path on either side, their twisted trunks and roots forming an eerie corridor. Elephant-ear sized leaves swayed in the wind, a dark emerald that gleamed in the light.

Jungle animals howled, and enormous lightning bugs flitted along the path. They were too big to be regular bugs, so they were most likely some kind of fairy, but I wasn't going to stop to investigate. There were dangerous creatures in the jungle at night—one of the reasons we hadn't wanted to go now—and in our world, fairies could be considered dangerous.

Especially if you called them lightning bugs.

A roar sounded in the distance, echoing through the jungle and making the leaves rustle on either side as small animals scurried for safety.

The roar came again, only closer.

Then another, and another.

"Oh shit," I muttered. This was bad.

~~~

Join my mailing list at www.linseyhall.com/subscribe to get a free copy of *Hidden Magic.* No spam and you can leave anytime!

AUTHOR'S NOTE

Thanks for reading *Attack by Magic!* The author's note is where I normally talk about the history and mythology in the book, and *Attack by Magic* had plenty of it.

To start, Oya, the mercenary leader in the beginning of the book, is based off an African goddess of the Yoruba people. In Yoruba, her name means "she tore", and she is a warrior associated with winds, lightning, death, and rebirth.

Cocidius is another Celtic war god, not dissimilar from Belatucadros. The Celtic culture spread all over Europe during the Iron Age, and as a result, there are many different gods from different regions that represent basically the same thing. I had quite a few Celtic war gods to choose from, but I chose Cocidius because he was worshipped in roughly the same place as Belatucadros—around Hadrian's Wall in the north of England.

The carved design of the man holding the sword and shield that Dr. G found in the *Attack by Magic* are based off of actual carvings that have been discovered of Cocidius around Hadrian's Wall. The fortress that they visit in the book is based off of the fort at Bewcastle in western England, which was originally a Roman fort associated with the worship of Cocidius. The

Romans called it *Fanum Cocidi*—The Shrine of Cocidius. Bree notes that there are mounds of earth—these were once Roman defenses. Over time, a castle was built and the fort fell into disrepair and took on other uses.

When Bree and Cade visited Cocidius's half realm, they noted that there were massive trees all around—far bigger than what is common in England today. The reason for this is one of the most interesting points in history. During the 16th and 17th century, the Royal Navy was so massive and powerful that they quickly decimated all the large forests in England in search of trees to build their ships. Many of their colonies were formed (at least in part) for the purpose of finding more timber for their ships. The Massachusetts Bay Charter of 1691 talks specifically about the trees belonging to the crown.

The fancy hotel and bar that Cade and Bree visited in Ghent was based on 1898 The Post, a hotel and bar that is currently housed in the old Post Office building. Gravensteen Castle is in fact located on one of the rivers, but there is no secret entrance to the underground harbor with a torture chamber (that I know of). There is a torture museum in the castle, which used to be located in the basement, and it's pretty horrifying. As with many large castles in Europe, it had a varied history after it was no longer used as a defensive stronghold. After it was abandoned in the 14th century, it was used as a courthouse, factory, prison, and even split up into houses. The castle underwent renovations in the late 19th century (a period when other similar castles were being renovated due to increased interest in history) and is currently an amazing place to visit.

The riddle that they encountered on the stairs in the castle is an old riddle from 18th century England. I found it while hunting for old riddles online (I like to use historic ones whenever possible), but it rang a bell in my head as being vaguely familiar. Then I placed it—the riddle was featured in *Die Hard 3*. It is a riddle that can be hissed very quickly and can sound quite threatening, so it was perfect for *Attack by Magic*.

Well, that's it for now. Hopefully I didn't miss any other historic elements. Thank you again for reading the books, and I hope you'll stick with Bree, Ana, and Rowan throughout their adventures!

ACKNOWLEDGMENTS

Thank you, Ben, for everything. There would be no books without you.

Thank you to Lindsey Loucks and Jena O'Connor for your excellent editing. The book is immensely better because of you! And thank you Eleonora, for your keen eye in spotting errors and for helping me with the Dutch translations. And also for advising me to visit Ghent—without you, we'd have no scene set in that fabulous city! And thank you Richard, for your keen error spotting.

Thank you to Orina Kafe for the beautiful cover art. Thank you to Collette Markwardt for allowing me to borrow the Pugs of Destruction, who are real dogs named Chaos, Havoc, and Ruckus. They were all adopted from rescue agencies.

GLOSSARY

Alpha Council - There are two governments that enforce law for supernaturals—the Alpha Council and the Order of the Magica. The Alpha Council governs all shifters. They work cooperatively with the Alpha Council when necessary—for example, when capturing FireSouls.

Blood Sorcerer - A type of Magica who can create magic using blood.

Dark Magic - The kind that is meant to harm. It's not necessarily bad, but it often is.

Demons - Often employed to do evil. They live in various hells but can be released upon the earth if you know how to get to them and then get them out. If they are killed on Earth, they are sent back to their hell.

Dragon Sense - A FireSoul's ability to find treasure. It is an internal sense that pulls them toward what they seek. It is easiest to find gold, but they can find anything or anyone that is valued by someone.

Djinn - Possesses invisibility and the ability to possess others for brief periods of time.

Earthwalking Gods - Reincarnates of the ancient gods who

can walk upon the earth. They are mortal but with all the power of that god.

Eclektica - A jack-of-all-trades who deals in spells.

Enchanted Artifacts – Artifacts can be imbued with magic that lasts after the death of the person who put the magic into the artifact (unlike a spell that has not been put into an artifact —these spells disappear after the Magica's death). But magic is not stable. After a period of time—hundreds or thousands of years depending on the circumstance—the magic will degrade. Eventually, it can go bad and cause many problems.

Fire Mage – A mage who can control fire.

FireSoul - A very rare type of Magica who shares a piece of the dragon's soul. They can locate treasure and steal the gifts (powers) of other supernaturals. With practice, they can manipulate the gifts they steal, becoming the strongest of that gift. They are despised and feared. If they are caught, they are thrown in the Prison of Magical Deviants.

The Great Peace - The most powerful piece of magic ever created. It hides magic from the eyes of humans.

Magica - Any supernatural who has the power to create magic—witches, sorcerers, mages. All are governed by the Order of the Magica.

Order of the Magica - There are two governments that enforce law for supernaturals—the Alpha Council and the Order of the Magica. The Order of the Magica govern all Magica. They work cooperatively with the Alpha Council when necessary—for example, when capturing FireSouls.

Seeker - A type of supernatural who can find things. FireSouls often pass off their dragon sense as Seeker power.

Seklie - Sea creatures lived off the coasts of Ireland and Scotland. They are seals who can also become human and draw their magic from the sea.

Shifter - A supernatural who can turn into an animal. All are governed by the Alpha Council.

Transporter - A type of supernatural who can travel anywhere. Their power is limited and must regenerate after each use.

Undercover Protectorate - A secret organization dedicated to protecting supernaturals and solving the crimes that no one else will.

Vampire - Blood drinking supernaturals with great strength and speed who live in a separate realm.

ABOUT LINSEY

Before becoming a writer, Linsey Hall was a nautical archaeologist who studied shipwrecks from Hawaii and the Yukon to the UK and the Mediterranean. She credits fantasy and historical romances with her love of history and her career as an archaeologist. After a decade of tromping around the globe in search of old bits of stuff that people left lying about, she settled down and started penning her own romance novels. Her Dragon's Gift series draws upon her love of history and the paranormal elements that she can't help but include.

COPYRIGHT

Copyright 2017 by Linsey Hall
Published by Bonnie Doon Press LLC

Linsey@LinseyHall.com
www.LinseyHall.com
https://www.facebook.com/LinseyHallAuthor
ISBN 978-1-942085-55-3